AGENTS OF FATE

TONY CONTRATTO

The First Book of
The Agents of Fate Series

Hensley de Vere Press

Lake Havasu City, AZ

ISBN 979-8-98860900-1 (Paperback)
ISBN 979-8-98860901-8 (Hardcover)
ISBN 979-8-98860902-5 (Ebook)

Library of Congress Control Number: 2023912312

First paperback and e-book editions July 2023
First hardcover edition July 2023

This book is a work of fiction. The story, all names, places, characters, and incidents portrayed in this work are products of the author's imagination or are used fictitiously. No identification with actual persons (living or deceased), places, locales, buildings, and products is intended or should be inferred.

Cover photo by Dino Reichmuth
Edited by Kim Beckham

Printed in the United States of America

Hensley de Vere Press LLC
1799 Kiowa Ave
Suite 111
Lake Havasu City, AZ 86403
hensleydevere.com
contact@hensleydevere.com

Dedication

Kayla, thank you for everything you do to make my world better.

To everyone else, that, at one point or another, said or did something that inspired me to continue writing… whether you knew it or not.

Richard, Anita, Edward, and Priscilla

Randy, Judy, Adam, Jennifer, Lacie, Emma

Lewis, Teresa, Alyssa, Kayla, Cody, Brenden

Kim Beckham

In Memory of Edward L Whitlow

MCMXXXVII - MMXIV

CONTENTS

برق

Chapter One

Of Death and Dreams

The alleyway had a peculiar stench. Sort of like three-day-old trash, feral cat, and alcoholic transient mixed together. It's really odd what you notice when you're running for your life. At least, that's what Christopher was thinking as he took a momentary pause to catch his breath while hiding behind some trash cans in the dark corner of a loading dock.

Looking at his surroundings, Christopher noted that the alley seemed clear of any visible life except for a small cat walking on a fire escape four stories above. A few moments passed without activity, but those mere seconds felt like minutes to Christopher. Exhaustion was skewing his perception of time. Had he finally lost his pursuer? Before Christopher could rejoice in that possibility, a hooded figure rounded the corner at the far end of the alley and answered his question. After pausing to look for its target, the figure began to approach. Christopher hesitated momentarily, weighing his options, then rose to his feet and began to run again. Immediately, the hooded figure gave chase.

Christopher rounded the next corner, stumbling over a rogue trash can that someone had thoughtlessly placed in the middle of the path. However, with adrenaline coursing through his veins, it didn't take long for him to reach a full sprint again. Cutting around the next corner, he looked back over his shoulder. It seemed that he was finally getting away.

At the end of this alleyway, the city streets were once again in view. If he could just make it to the road, Christopher hypothesized that he could blend in with the crowd and disappear. Perhaps he would hop in a cab and speed off to safety. Anything other than running through these stupid alleys.

"Why the hell did I cut into the alleys in the first place?" he asked himself.

No matter; the street was within reach now. Only a hundred or so feet remained between Christopher and freedom. Once again, looking over his shoulder, the hooded figure was now nowhere in sight. As he approached the boulevard, his sprint slowed to a walk. The busy street seemed safe and inviting. Never before had he felt such comfort from the organized chaos of downtown. After catching his bearings for a moment, Christopher turned to his right and began walking down the street. It was a street that he had been on only a few times in his life, so he was only pretty sure that he was walking in the right direction.

After a couple of blocks, the scenery became more familiar; a small coffee shop where he had gone on a date with a girl that led to a short relationship that didn't quite work out, a Chinese restaurant his buddy Jason always raved about, and finally a pet shop where his sister bought her over-affectionate cat. Now he knew that he was on the right track again.

With each passing memory, comfort again flowed through his body. Strangers passed in the opposite direction without incident, so Christopher gave no thought to the approaching figure. A woman, perhaps, dressed in a flowing black coat. As the figure got closer, her pace slowed, and she walked directly toward Christopher. A quick surge of adrenaline kicked through Christopher's veins as the woman stopped precisely in front of him. She drew something from her coat pocket, but by the time Christopher recognized what it was, the object was already pointing its deadly gaze right at him.

As the flood of epinephrine told his brain that it was fight or flight time, a deafening blast cut through the air. The unexpected sound stopped pedestrians and vehicles alike in their paths. The screams of onlookers were dulled by the brutal warmth and agonizing pain in Christopher's chest. As he looked down for further analysis, his suspicion was confirmed by a profusely bleeding gunshot wound. Christopher fell to the ground, clutching at his chest.

A woman on the opposite side of the street cried out. "Oh my God! He's been shot!" Some of the nearby crowd ran in fear for their safety, while some began to rush toward the scene to help.

As the young man's eyes closed and his breathing slowed, he caught a glimpse of his assailant. A blonde girl, maybe only twenty years of age.. pretty… not someone you would expect to be a cold-blooded killer. He drew his last breath and passed away. A faint aura of light seemed to rise from his lifeless body and ascend into the night sky.

The girl had run off into the nearby alley just as a group of bystanders reached the young man. They called 911 and tried to resuscitate him, with no success. A small group of men that had come over to help ran down the alley to look for the suspect. They returned a few minutes later empty-handed. Several police cruisers, accompanied by an ambulance, arrived shortly thereafter. The first responders descended en masse on the scene.

ↄ ↄ ↄ ↄ ↄ ↄ

Hayden awoke suddenly, sweating and in a panic. Though he hadn't been, his hands tingled like he had been sleeping on them. Hayden sat up in his bed and pondered the intense dream he had just had. "Who were those people," he wondered as he sat silently, staring off into the darkness of the room. Some dreams came and went, but this one was vivid, and he remembered it fully like it was etched in his mind.

Hayden looked over at the clock… 6:30 a.m. It was just about time to get up for class anyway. He rose from his bed and began his morning routine. A quick shower and a bagel for breakfast. He threw on some clothes and made his way out the door, this dream lingering in the back of his mind the entire time. Who was that girl? It sort of reminded him of his best friend, well, at least in the short glimpse he saw of her. Finally, he brushed it off as he jumped into his car and headed toward the university.

Back again… Cal State Fullerton, in the heart of Orange County, California. He had been attending for about three years now. His major was Biochemistry, with a minor in Pre-Med Studies. As he got out of his vehicle and made his way to McCarthy Hall for his first morning class, the feeling hit him… it was a sensation that he had dealt with for as long as he could remember. His vision blurred for a moment, an intense chill ran down his spine, and it almost felt like that chill flowed out from his body like energy. It was just normal to him now, something that happened occasionally. At first, when he told his parents about it as a child, they promptly took him to the doctor's office to have him checked out. The doctor found nothing wrong with him and dismissed it as growing pains or some such thing. He said it should go away with time. It didn't go away, but Hayden just lived with it. There was no actual harm, just that weird feeling every once in a while.

He arrived at his Physiology class and took his usual seat. The course flew by, and the day wore on. Soon he found himself at a local bar and grill with some friends for dinner and drinks. His best friend Paige sat beside him. She was an amiable and outgoing girl. Blonde, with a style that was kind of unique. She didn't present herself like she was trying to draw attention, but she got it nonetheless. Several of their other friends sat around the table, all enjoying drinks and conversation. Hayden ordered a round of tequila shots for the table, as was customary whenever he or his friend Dan showed up… and Dan had just walked into the bar right on cue.

"To another day of classes over and another night of revelry!" Hayden toasted.

The table full of friends took their shots and continued discussing their day and plans for an upcoming get-together at Dan's apartment. Dan wanted to celebrate the approaching end of the semester with a bang, but in reality, it was just an excuse to get another party going for themselves and their larger circle of friends. The reason could have been that it was a Saturday night for all they cared.

"So yeah, just show up at like 8:00 p.m. and bring some drinks. Same as usual," Dan said.

"It sucks I won't be able to come," Paige replied. "Vacation time with the family."

"Yeah, where are you going again?" Dan asked.

"Just up to Yosemite for camping and hiking," Paige responded.

"Well, have loads of fun out there. We'll have a drink in your honor," Dan joked.

"Yeah, thanks!" Paige said sarcastically. "Keep an eye on Hayden, don't let him get too crazy."

"Isn't that the point?" Hayden interjected, causing Dan to raise his glass in a mock toast.

Hayden stepped outside to the bar's patio to light up a smoke. At this point, he was feeling the effects of the alcohol in his system. He wasn't drunk just yet but had a decent buzz going on. As he lit the end of his cigarette, he looked out onto the world. The crescent moon hung over the sky, and the stars shone across the vast darkness like torches. The trees across the boulevard were draped over the random people walking to their destinations. The chill ran down his spine again and his vision began to blur. The feelings were intensifying and he felt a deeper connection to everything... and everyone. Like a power deep inside him, flowing out into the night sky. As if it all had a meaning that he didn't quite understand yet. He let out the last puff of smoke as Paige walked out to meet him.

"What ya thinking about?" she asked.

"Well, now that you mention it... a dream I had last night," he paused. "It was the most intense dream I've ever had. I don't even know who the people were, but it was like I was watching real life unfold. The guy was running for his life and being chased by this girl. She killed him... and then I woke up."

"Wow, that's quite a dream there. Maybe all those classes you're taking are messing with your brain," Paige jokingly responded.

"Yeah, probably!" Hayden said with a chuckle. "It's just been in my mind all day." He didn't mention that the murderous girl in the dream resembled her, not that it was of any real consequence to him. People usually dream of others they know, he thought.

"Well, let's head back in for another round," she said. "Don't wanna kill the buzz, right?"

"That's for sure!" Hayden replied. They headed back inside the bar and took a shot of Fireball that was waiting for them. The cinnamon whiskey warmed his throat and led the way to several more shots and beers. The night blurred forward, and soon he was in his bed. He shut his eyes on another day.

◌ ◌ ◌ ◌ ◌ ◌

Friday finally came around, and Hayden found himself over at Paige's parent's house as her family packed for their impending trip to Yosemite for the weekend. Paige and Hayden sat in her old bedroom talking until it was finally time for her to depart. As Paige and her family loaded into their car, Hayden said his goodbyes and then drove back to his apartment.

After a seemingly endless drive, Paige and her family reached their campsite in Yosemite and began to set up camp. The evening was mild and clear, so Paige and her father took a short hike close to their site to enjoy the last remnants of the daylight. They returned to camp about an hour later, and Paige's mother had dinner ready. The family ate and then spent several hours talking as they looked up at the stars in the clear night sky. Paige was glad to have a nice, relaxing trip away from the stresses of life in college, which she went on and on about during the conversation with her parents around the small fire they had built. As midnight neared, Paige and her parents piled into their respective tents. The family was going to get up early and head out on a long hike the following day.

Paige was restless that night, even though the short hike and the long car ride had seemingly worn her out. Eventually, she fell asleep to the sounds of a nearby stream and the incessant chirping of crickets in the distance. When she was awakened by her mother several hours later, it seemed all too soon. Indeed it was 7:00 a.m., and breakfast was already waiting for her. After a quick breakfast of omelets, which her father always made in little plastic baggies dunked in boiling water on the camp stove and some grilled potatoes, the family set out on their morning hike. Paige's father had done some pre-vacation research and wanted to try out a hike he had read about online. Although the hike in question was rather long, Paige and her mother agreed to go when they saw how excited Paige's father was about it. Paige had always enjoyed hiking anyway; her father, sister, and she had always adventured out at least once a month when they all lived under the same roof. While they mostly hiked around the local spots, they occasionally branched out to neighboring towns to mix it up. Paige realized she hadn't done much hiking since moving to college. As she enjoyed the last few bites of breakfast, she felt increasingly invigorated for what she deemed a long-overdue reconnection with nature.

Paige's father led the way, setting off toward the nearest mountain. Once they reached the foothills, the family stopped to rest. Paige wandered off to explore a little by herself while her mother and father sat down and continued to take a breather. As she ventured off, Paige followed a small stream up into the foothills of the towering mountain before her. The stream continued until it seemingly disappeared into the mountainside. She sat on a nearby rock and admired the exceptional scenery around her. The fir and oak trees filled the surrounding wooded area, and small animals scurried about on their day-to-day business.

As Paige marveled at the beauty of the environment, her eyes were eventually drawn to a small opening in the mountainside. She wasn't sure if it even was an opening. As Paige focused more intently, the crack in the rock almost resembled an optical illusion. She decided to investigate and walked through the gap in the mountain that was just barely big enough for her to squeeze through. As she entered, she was amazed to find a large cavernous space. In the middle of the room was a large slab of rock that almost resembled a long rectangular table. The walls were sparsely lined with an orange rock that almost seemed to glow in the dimly lit room.

She approached the slab in the center of the room and examined it. It had carvings all around the side that appeared to have been there for some time. She couldn't distinguish what language they were or if they were a language. The top of the slab was smooth and covered in a light sprinkling of dust. It didn't appear that anyone had been here in some time. Paige walked to the wall nearest her and looked at the strange orange rock jutting from the side of the stone. It seemed that its intensity grew as she came closer to it.

As Paige reached out her hand to feel this orange rock, she heard a rustle behind her. She looked back hurriedly, only to find nothing else in the room with her. Relieved, she once again turned her attention to the strange rocks. The noise repeated, and this time it seemed closer to her. Now scared, she turned to find a dark figure before her. Panic set in, but before she could say or do anything, a sudden blow to her head sent her into a world of unconscious darkness.

______

Paige awoke a short time later. She wasn't sure how long she'd been out, but now she found herself lying on the large slab of stone in the middle of the room. Though she wasn't bound with rope or anything of the sort, she found that she couldn't move her body at all.

"Hello, is anyone there?" she asked, her voice shaking with fear.

Nothing… and then a few minutes later, the dark figure approached as if from out of nowhere. Paige couldn't make out any features at all. It was like this thing was all darkness, in a roughly human form. It hovered over her and seemed to be looking down at her. Paige was terrified, but she still could not move despite every attempt that her mind made to tell her body to get up and run. The dark figure reached its arms down to the side of the slab and produced a glowing dagger. Now Paige was frantic… What was happening? How did she get herself into this? A million thoughts were running through her mind all at once.

"Please, no!" she pleaded. "I'm sorry I came in here. I'll leave and never come back."

The figure ignored her words and drew the dagger over Paige's body. She flinched as she saw the downward thrust begin. The blade slid effortlessly through the flesh of her chest. Paige screamed in excruciating pain as the dagger continued through her body until the tip of it was pressed against the stone slab underneath her. She could feel the blood pouring from the wound as the dagger was removed from her chest. The dark figure stood over Paige, watching blood pour down the sides of the slab. Paige's vision began to darken and blur as she slipped from consciousness. Her heart stopped beating…

Awake. Paige arose from the cold slab on which several liters of her blood had, just minutes before, been drained from her body via a stab wound. She breathed in a deep gasping breath and looked around the room.

Moments earlier, the shadowy figure responsible for her fatal injuries had introduced its darkness into her being. As Paige took her last breath, the figure hovered over her, and its form became like a dark fog. The orange rocks lining the cave walls began to glow intensely as Paige's soul departed from her body. The shadowy fog twisted around her soul as it hung over her, intermingling with and permeating her essence. The mixture of the dark fog and her soul then rushed back into her body through her mouth and nose. This *thing* had taken residence within her.

"Hi, I'm Paige," she said as she stood up from the slab, her slightly distorted voice echoing against the cave walls. She repeated the phrase several times until it sounded correct. The darkness within her now had the ability to take over her

———

mind and actions at any time, always present and able to use her memories and personality.

Paige walked across the cavern to the exit. As she emerged, she looked down at herself and inspected her appearance. Blood still soaked her shirt. This wouldn't do. She walked to the nearby stream and removed her shirt and bra, tossing them aside. Paige washed the blood from her body and out of her hair. The stab wound, which had pierced her between two ribs just below her left breast, appeared to be healed now. She walked down along the stream to where her backpack was sitting and retrieved a sports bra and a new shirt, which she put on. She then began the roughly one-mile trek back to where her parents were still resting.

"Hey, there you are!" her father said as Paige appeared in sight. "We were beginning to wonder where you wandered off to."

"Oh yeah, sorry, I went a little further than I thought and got turned around. Then I snagged my shirt on some thorns and had to change it," Paige replied.

"Find anything interesting out that way?"

"Not really, just more trees and squirrels."

"Well, I guess let's get going again," her father recommended.

They grabbed their gear and set out again on the

remainder of their hike. They returned to camp several hours later.

The family stayed up late into the night. Paige's father told stories of camping trips from his childhood that he had taken with his father and brother. They cooked s'mores around the campfire after dinner and listened to some music. As the night wore on, they retired to the tents and went to sleep.

About an hour later, Paige's eyes opened suddenly. She rose from her sleeping bag. The night was dead quiet and pitch dark. She reached over beside her into her duffle bag and grabbed some clothes. She exited the tent and stood outside next to the now almost non-existent campfire, just embers glowing in the slight breeze. She was driven to do something… now, in the middle of the night, though she didn't know what.

Paige stripped off her pajama shirt and shorts. It was late in the month of May, but the temperature was still only in the forties this late at night. She noticed the cold air chilling her naked body as she stood there. Paige was frozen in place, as if in a trance, by the fire pit, like she was waiting for instructions on what to do. No one was up or around to witness her strikingly odd behavior, but even if there had been, she probably wouldn't have noticed.

Several minutes went by. Suddenly, Paige came back to reality and looked down at herself. Goosebumps covered every inch of her body from the chilly air. She took the clothes she had grabbed from her duffle bag and put them on… a long-sleeve shirt, a pair of black leggings, and her favorite long black coat. She then walked westward into the forest.

The next thing Paige noticed, she had arrived in a city. She didn't know what city she was in or how she got there… That was all a blur. It was still dark out, so she figured there was no way she could have walked all that way, but she had no recollection of anything between the campfire and this moment. Paige strolled down the city sidewalk and looked around at her surroundings. Even in the late hour, pedestrians and cars still bustled about. Paige took a turn and made her way into an alley, where she caught a glimpse of a twenty-something-year-old man in the distance walking toward her. Suddenly, as if she was being commanded by an unseen force, she knew what she was here to do. Paige pulled the hood of her jacket up, concealing her hair. She had found her target.

Paige's hands were sore and stained with dried blood. She vaguely recalled cutting herself on glass… and flashes of breaking into a house along her way to her destination. Still hazily remembering bits and pieces of how she arrived here, she instinctively reached down into the pocket of her coat.

Her bloodied hand found the cold grip of a small handgun that had been the plunder of her burglary.

"The gun… this must have been why I broke into that house," Paige thought to herself.

As Paige walked through the alley, she felt a steadily growing force clouding her mind and weighing on her body. It felt like a darkness was swirling in her soul and coming to life, dampening her emotions and honing her reflexes toward a single purpose.

The young man continued his stride through the alley toward Paige, dividing his attention between his cell phone and his intended path. As he and Paige closed the distance between them, he looked up in her direction. Paige locked eyes with him for several seconds and drew her hand from her coat pocket. His gaze switched from Paige's indistinguishable facial features to her hand and the weapon she was now wielding. Immediately, he stopped his forward momentum and attempted to speak but only managed to mumble an unintelligible group of sounds in a confused plea. As Paige's hand began to rise from her side, he turned and stumbled for a moment, but the adrenaline quickly began to course through his system, and he took off in a sprint away from Paige. He heard an echoing pop as Paige fired a round in his direction. With about thirty yards between them, her shot had missed… but he felt small brick fragments pelting the side of his head from the building wall the bullet hit.

As he turned a corner, he slid and stumbled again. Paige started to give chase. He rose to his feet and put some distance between Paige and himself, turning another corner, this time managing to stay on his feet. Slowing his pace, the young man looked over his shoulder and noticed he no longer saw her. He looked at his surroundings and found a dimly lit corner of a loading dock with some trash cans. He might be able to hide himself well enough here and then get away. He decided to take the chance before Paige caught up to him. He ducked down behind the trash cans and convinced himself he was out of sight, though he couldn't help but think that his breathing was as loud as a freight train and would surely give him away. He sat there for several moments, trying to remain perfectly still and quiet. Paige rounded the corner. He held his breath…

Paige looked around the alleyway for any signs of the young man. She noticed slurred footprints in the mud and debris heading toward the nearby loading dock and started walking that way. Suddenly, she saw the man dart from behind a grouping of trash cans and take off running again. She continued her chase but didn't have a chance to get off another shot before he disappeared behind an adjacent building.

As Paige rounded the corner, she saw the young man heading towards the city streets. She abandoned the chase and ran down an intersecting alley to intercept him. The young man's false sense of security after having reached the assumed safety of the sidewalk betrayed him. As Paige stepped out of the alleys, she opened her coat and pulled the hood back down. Paige quickly spotted the young man amongst a small crowd of approaching pedestrians. Once they were within ten feet of each other, Paige slowed her stroll to a near standstill. She gazed into his eyes as she drew the gun from her pocket.

Now with the darkness inside her in complete control, Paige savored the look of fear that flashed over his enlarged pupils as he realized she was his pursuer. After pulling the trigger, Paige stood on the sidewalk looking over the young man lying on the ground beneath her. He was clutching at his chest in desperate confusion. She listened in triumphant silence to the gurgle in his breathing as she watched a pool of blood form underneath him. Paige stared at him with an empty gaze as he drew his final breath. She faintly noticed a scream in the distance and the sound of people clamoring in her direction. She regained her composure and sprinted into the darkness of the alleyways again.

ظل

Chapter Two

Friends and Enemies

Paige sat uncomfortably at her desk in her afternoon Sociology class. The professor rambled on some facts and statistics on urban planning and the use of the grid system for street design during the westward expansion of the United States. Paige wasn't paying attention, but the words bounced around in the back of her mind before exiting her memory. She felt disconnected… from her classmates, from her friends, and from the reality she knew. The foreboding feeling of darkness that she had felt in the city's alleyways still lurked within her, clouding her mood and her ambition to participate in any activities she would typically enjoy.

"Paige, you can go now…" she faintly heard the professor say.

She zoned back into the moment and looked around

the classroom. She was the only student left in the room. "How am I that out of it?" she thought.

"Oh. Sorry, Professor Dupree, I guess I zoned out for a minute there," Paige responded.

"No problem," Dupree replied with a chuckle. "Just remember to submit your essay by Friday, and we'll be just fine."

Paige nodded in agreement with him and stood up from her desk, grabbing her backpack and purse. She walked out into the hallway and checked her cell phone. Dan had texted to let her know that everyone was meeting up for dinner at Eduardo Quesada's, a nearby Mexican restaurant, in about forty minutes.

"Okay, sounds good," she texted back to him and shoved her phone away in her back pocket.

Paige walked through the campus and across the street to her one-bedroom apartment. She had thirty minutes left to meet everyone at the restaurant for dinner, which was only a two-minute walk from her place. "Plenty of time to freshen up a bit," Paige told herself. She walked into the bathroom and took her clothes off, throwing them into a crumpled pile in the corner with several other pairs from days previous. Paige turned on the shower and waited for the water to warm as she looked at herself in the mirror. Her body looked the same, and she recognized her reflection, but her mind still felt as if it were disconnected from herself. Paige looked down at her hands, again noticing they were still quite freshly injured.

Paige stepped into the hot water of the shower and washed her body. She skipped her hair, however, as she didn't have that much time to prepare. As she finished rinsing her body, Paige shut off the shower and dried herself as she proceeded to her bedroom. Her outfit wasn't given much thought; she just threw on whatever she found first in the closet that somewhat matched. She put her hair up in a messy bun and touched up her makeup in the mirror hanging on her bedroom door.

Paige exited her apartment and soon arrived at the restaurant. She walked in through the lobby area, taking note of the familiar scene, the bright colors, and the somewhat eccentric use of sombreros and maracas as decoration. As Paige passed into the dining area, she was welcomed by the greeting of Dan, Hayden, and their other shared friends, Clark, Abby, and Samantha. As she walked to the table, Paige noted that they were all in their usual post-classes jovial mood. She attempted to appear engaged in the group dynamic as she sat down.

"What's up, Paige? How was your 'soc' class?" Hayden asked her as she took her seat at the table.

"Oh, it was okay. Just the usual lecture and an essay assignment," Paige replied, her voice monotone and slightly trailing off quietly at the end of the sentence.

"Bruh, you okay?" Dan interjected, noticing Paige's unenthusiastic response.

"Ummm… yeah… Just a little out of it today, I guess," Paige replied while staring down at the menu in front of her.

"Yeah, I guess so…" Dan murmured. "Like why are you looking at the menu when you order the same thing every time we're here?"

"Dan!" Abby said aggressively. "Uncalled for, dude… she said she's had a rough day, don't be an ass," Abby's aggressive tone now lightened with a slight laugh.

"Whoa, okay… I just haven't had any tequila yet. Chill out, Abby," Dan joked back at her. "It's all good, Paige. We can order for you also if you're going to zone out the entire time," Dan said, now directing his attempted humor at Paige.

Hayden reached over and touched Paige's arm.

"Do you want anything to drink to drown out the memory of your classes?" Hayden asked her, with concern and empathy in his voice.

Paige woke from her daze when she felt Hayden's touch. There was a faint odd feeling she had never felt before when his hand made contact with her. She didn't know quite what it was and thus quickly dismissed it, now noticing that she had been the epitome of awkward since she arrived.

"Ummm.. yeah. I'll have a rum and Coke," she told Hayden, her voice now alive with some of its usual inflection and tone.

"Alright, that's more like it! Coming right up," Hayden replied as he stood up and walked to the bar.

The night waned on, and Paige caught herself several times again slipping back and forth between mentally present and lost in her own mind. Samantha had left the restaurant already since she had an early class the following day. Paige excused herself to the bathroom, where she stood again in front of a mirror, gazing at herself for several minutes. She rinsed her face in the sink and closed her eyes to try to snap herself back into reality.

Paige opened her eyes. To her surprise, she saw the night sky above her. She looked around, confused, and found that she was lying in the tall grass of an open field in a place wholly unfamiliar to her. She could hear voices far off in the distance with a seemingly frantic cadence. Paige stood up, gathered herself for a moment, and then looked around the field. To her surprise, she saw the body of a young man ly-ing about twenty feet away from her, covered in blood. She approached the body and gazed down at him as if trying to remember something about what had happened. The young man's eyes were open, and he stared off into the sky, his face still etched with a look of terrifying fear… his last emotions and thoughts seemed to be eternally captured in his expression. Paige stepped backward from the body, stumbling on a rock behind her and falling to the ground as she processed the scene. She barely caught herself with her hands before hitting the ground full force and then hurriedly rose to her feet again. Her thoughts were interrupted by the sound of the voices she had heard before growing louder and closer. She looked behind her to see the beams of several flashlights bouncing from the ground to the sky as their carriers quickly moved through the grasses toward Paige. "No more time to spend here," she thought, running in the opposite direction. Paige had no clue where she was, but she knew that her location looked like nothing that was familiar to her. She ran until her lungs felt like they were being seared with flames, and then she fell to her knees. Her vision went black, and she lost consciousness.

ೞ ೞ ೞ ೞ ೞ ೞ

Paige awoke suddenly to the sound of pounding on a door. She jumped from her sleep and opened her eyes wide with the sudden jolt of waking adrenaline. The pounding at the door started again. Paige looked around and found that she was in her bed, in her own apartment… She was nude, lying on top of her blankets. As she examined herself further, she found that her knees were dirty and bruised and several reeds of grass were strewn throughout her total disaster of a hair-do.

"What the absolute fuck?" Paige thought to herself.

As she rose from her bed, she immediately noticed the fatigue in her muscles and the pain in her joints, as if her body wanted to give out on her. She grabbed onto her desk to prevent herself from toppling over on the floor. Again the pounding on the front door of her apartment started up.

Paige looked around her room for something to wear, now properly awake and not panicking. She walked to her dresser and quickly pulled on a pair of panties and pajama shorts. Paige promptly grabbed the first oversized tee shirt she could find so that she could forgo putting on a bra. She had no clue who was banging on her front door like the world was ending, so she wanted to at least look a fraction of the way presentable. On the way out of her bedroom, Paige quickly looked in her mirror. "Fuck, I look like a train hit me," she thought, now altogether regretting the decision to look in the mirror. She quickly tried to pull most of the grass from her tangled hair as she continued down the hallway toward the front door. The loud knocking continued.

"Fucking shit, I'm coming! Stop knocking like the fucking police!" she yelled as she approached the door.

Paige violently swung the front door of her apartment open with a combination of anger, panic, and readiness to fight someone. She found Dan standing outside her door, his fist still raised in the air, ready to fire off another brutal salvo of deafening knocking.

"Dude, what the fuck?!" Paige asked Dan, with a blatantly obvious tone of exasperation.

"No…. You, dude, what the fuck?" Dan replied flatly.

"What?" Paige quipped back at him.

"Are you, like, not okay?" Dan asked. "You got up from the table last night to go to the bathroom, and then we never saw you again. Hayden tried to call you, and your phone was off… he walked over here, and you weren't home. So, again, what the fuck, Paige?"

"I… I don't know, Dan," Paige replied, now letting her guard down and relaxing her tone. "I remember going to the bathroom, and I remember standing there looking at myself in the mirror. The next thing I remember, literally, is waking up to you pounding on my front door."

"Whoa, really?" Dan said, surprised. "You didn't even have that much to drink last night. What happened?"

"Honestly, I have no clue," Paige said. "Do you want to come in?"

"No, I gotta get to my first class like right now," Dan answered. "I just wanted to come by and check your place one more time. I'll text Hayden and tell him you're alive, but you should probably call him soon. He was kind of pissed."

"Shit, yeah… I will," Paige said with a sigh.

"Okay, I'll catch up with you later on," Dan told her as he started to walk away, then humorously shouted back to her. "Glad to know you didn't get abducted!"

Paige closed the door and locked it. She looked up toward the ceiling and let out another long sigh. Her stomach was growling with the intensity of a hurricane, but she felt disgusting, so she put off breakfast. Paige walked down the hallway toward the bathroom, stripping her makeshift outfit off as she walked… tee shirt thrown on the edge of the couch, pajama shorts kicked off on the hallway carpet, and panties flung by her foot past the shorts almost into her bedroom.

"I'm so fucked…" Paige mumbled to herself as she started the shower.

Paige grabbed a makeup remover wipe and scrubbed the last remnants of her makeup off from the previous night as she loathed what her hair looked like in the mirror. She then attempted to brush out the tangles as the water warmed up. By the time her hair was halfway decent, the shower was steaming up over the glass doors. She stepped into the shower and let the hot water run down her body, instantly soothing her sore muscles. Paige continued her self-examination as she stood in the water's warmth for a while. She found that she had tiny cuts and irritation all along her arms, her neck, and on her chest from her collarbone to where the top edge of her bra cups would rest. As the dirt rinsed away from her knees, she could now clearly see the bruising mixed with spots of dried blood. The palms of her hands were also scraped up and sore.

Paige began washing herself, noticing more soreness in her body with every move she made. She completely abandoned the thought of shaving anything. After what seemed like an eternal fifteen minutes, she shut the shower off and walked to her bedroom, leaving a trail of water behind her as it dripped from her body. She patted herself dry with a towel that was draped over her desk chair and then proceeded to do a mediocre job of drying her hair with the towel. She was still tired, exhausted, really. Paige decided to nap for an hour or so before calling Hayden so she didn't feel so out of it.

Paige returned the towel to its place on her desk chair and went back and forth in her head between what would be the optimal balance of comfort and function regarding getting dressed. She ultimately erred on the side of comfort and decided on a minimal approach to clothing. She looked back to her bedroom doorway at the perfectly good pair of panties she had kicked off half an hour ago.

"Nope. Too far away, and I'm too sore to bend down and grab them," Paige told herself.

She walked over to her dresser drawer, grabbed a new pair, and pulled them on.

"Perfect outfit for right now," she mused.

She walked back toward her bed, ready to fall into it, when her stomach angrily reminded her that it had been empty for God knows how long. Paige groaned and grudgingly decided to walk to the kitchen. She shook her head and sighed as she walked past the pair of panties that, moments ago, she had firmly determined were too far away to bother retrieving.

"Guess you win this round," she mockingly said to the underwear as she passed them. "But I'm still not going to pick you up."

Paige wandered out to the kitchen and grabbed an English muffin from a bag on the counter. She waited for the toaster to bring the breakfast item to an appropriate level of toastiness and then slathered a sloppy glob of peanut butter between the two halves of the muffin. She took a bite and could feel her stomach thanking her as if she had pulled it from a certain death on the edge of a cliff. As Paige consumed the remainder of her breakfast, she sat on the couch. With the last bite, Paige sunk back into the cushions and felt the last bits of energy disappear from her body. She laid down across the couch cushions and dozed off to sleep.

ෆ ෆ ෆ ෆ ෆ ෆ

Hayden checked his phone to see that Dan had texted him.

"Hey, Paige is alive. She answered the door at her place. Looks like she was in a bar fight and lost. Omw to class," the text message read.

"Thanks bro. HMU after classes," Hayden typed back.

Hayden changed direction and walked southward down the hallway of University Hall. He noticed the lighting fixtures in the hallway were slightly swinging from the roof as if there had just been a tiny earthquake. He dismissed it and continued on his way outside, walking across the quad area toward the direction of Paige's apartment building. As he crossed the road in front of the university, he ran scenarios through his head of why Paige went AWOL the night before. Hayden couldn't come up with anything that made sense to him.

As Hayden approached the apartment complex where Paige lived, he sent off a quick text message to her that he was coming over. He opted to climb the stairs instead of taking the elevator since it was all the way at the other end of the hall and seemed to be the slowest elevator in existence. As he ascended the staircase, he checked his phone. Still no text back from Paige.

Hayden arrived at Paige's door and knocked with his usual rhythmic knock. No answer. He tried again and waited. Still no answer. Hayden let out an audible sigh and reached into his pocket. Paige and Hayden had keys to each other's apartments for emergencies or in case they needed a place to crash on the couch after a night out at one of the local bars.

Hayden pulled his keyring out and found the key… It was a bright pink bedazzled-looking thing that Paige thought would look funny on Hayden's keyring. He slid it into the keyhole and unlocked the door, knocking once more as he opened it.

"Paige, you in here?" Hayden asked in a louder-than-normal voice across a seemingly empty room.

There was no response as Hayden walked further in and noticed the peanut butter jar on the counter. He walked into the front room and was slightly surprised to find Paige passed out on her couch, dressed only in her panties, with a crumb-covered paper towel crumpled between her stomach and the cushion.

"Paige!" Hayden said this time, in an even louder voice, as he pushed on her shoulder.

Paige began to slowly and groggily awake from her impromptu resting place. As she opened her eyes and fought through the haze of waking up, she saw Hayden standing there with his arms crossed. She opened her eyes wider now and looked around. She first noted the sunlight flooding into the room from the window and then, as she rubbed her face with her hand, observed the fact that she was hardly clothed.

"Oh," Paige said raspily. "Wow… I must have really been out."

"That's possibly an understatement," Hayden replied.

Paige sat up, still letting her eyes adjust to the light. After a moment, she rose to her feet and again noticed the aching in her muscles. She breathed in and out heavily and then started walking toward the hallway.

"Oh my God, I feel like I could still sleep another eight hours," Paige said as she continued walking across the room. "Ugh, come to my bedroom so I can get dressed while you inevitably yell at me for disappearing last night."

Hayden followed her down the hallway to the bedroom and examined the scene of various pieces of clothing strewn about the floor. Paige walked over to her dresser.

"So, where did you disappear to last night?" Hayden asked.

Paige pulled some items from the dresser and turned back to face Hayden to answer him. A look of contemplation sat on her face as she thought about the answer. After a few moments of silence, she told Hayden the only thing she remembered.

"I honestly don't know…" Paige replied as she put on her bra and then slid on some comfortable shorts. She walked over to the closet to pick out a shirt.

"You weren't that drunk, were you? You don't remember anything? You weren't like drugged or anything, were you?" Hayden fired off questions in rapid succession.

Paige pulled the first shirt that semi-matched her shorts over her head and finished up her makeshift outfit. "No… I mean, I don't think I was drugged. I woke up here alone and don't remember being with anyone else last night after the restaurant. The last thing I remember is going to the bathroom and looking in the mirror. I remember feeling relatively fine at that moment. Then I don't remember anything after that until I woke up this morning."

"…and you're not like, hurt at all?" Hayden queried, the tone of his voice now turning delicate with concern.

Paige understood what Hayden was trying to ask. "I'm sore as hell all over like I got in a street fight… but no, I didn't get assaulted or anything," she replied.

"Okay… Thank God," Hayden said, as he ran both hands through his hair, then ran them down his neck, interlocking his fingers and holding that pose for a moment while letting out a sigh… still slightly frustrated by the situation, but also relieved that Paige insisted nothing nefarious had occurred. He followed her as she walked back down the hallway to the front room.

"Honestly, if I remember anything, I will tell you, Hayden… you know that," Paige said. "I'm just as interested as everyone else to know what happened, but I can't seem to remember anything for the life of me."

"Alright, I believe you," Hayden responded. "I was just worried; we all were. I guess we'll have to make sure you have a bathroom buddy next time we go out so you don't sneak away."

"For real," Paige said, laughing lightly. "I guess I need that."

❧ ❧ ❧ ❧ ❧ ❧

Paige slept on and off for the remainder of the day. When she finally decided to get up and stay out of bed, it was already 6:00 p.m.

"Great, now I've just screwed up my entire sleep schedule!" she thought.

She checked her phone and found a text message from Hayden that he had sent two hours ago asking if she wanted to join the group for an early dinner at 4:30.

"Dammit," she thought as she typed a quick response to Hayden's text, letting him know she had been sleeping.

"No problem," Hayden's reply text message came back. "I'll meet you tomorrow before class at the usual spot for breakfast."

Paige fired off one more text to Hayden, letting him know that she would be there for breakfast. Luckily, being close to campus put several quick options for food within walking distance of her apartment. Paige freshened up and made her way out the door to calm her growling stomach.

When she arrived back home, Paige decided to watch television and take some allergy medicine, hoping that the antihistamine would help her fall back to sleep for the night so she could try to salvage a regular sleep pattern. She flicked on an episode of The Golden Girls and settled into the couch.

Sleep came more expediently than Paige thought it would. However, only Paige's consciousness slept as the darkness inside her took control of her mind and body once again.

Paige got dressed and journeyed out of her apartment, ending up in Los Angeles outside Union Station at 10:30 p.m. She waited outside the station near the long-term parking structure near North Vignes Street.

Paige sat on a nearby park bench and silently admired the architecture of the surrounding buildings until a young woman began to approach. Paige rose from her seat and walked closer to the parking structure, making sure to stay out of the field of vision of passing cars and buses.

As the young woman was passing, Paige remarked. "I hear that Somerset gets pretty cold."

The woman stopped with a slightly confused look on her face as she took in Paige's appearance. "How did you know that I'm from Wisconsin?" she asked Paige. "Are you my cousin's friend that's here to pick me up?"

"Possibly," Paige replied. "You're Eva, right?"

"Yeah, Eva Oliversson," the woman replied, now more at ease. "My cousin is Charlie."

Paige faked a laugh. "Good ol' Charlie! Guess he had to work late or something," she improvised.

"Well, I'm just glad I don't have to take another bus," Eva said. "I'm ready to get back to Charlie's and get some sleep."

"Definitely," agreed Paige. "Here, let me grab your bag for you."

Eva smiled and thanked Paige for her generosity. Paige approached Eva with her left arm outstretched to take her carry-on-style suitcase. As Paige grabbed the suitcase with her left hand, she drew her right hand from the pocket of her hoodie. Paige's motions were so quick and fluid that Eva never noticed the knife until Paige had lunged it into her abdomen.

Paige dropped the suitcase and muffled Eva's scream with her hand. Paige pulled the knife out, and blood began to stain Eva's shirt. The initial feeling of shock was now beginning to be replaced with panic in Eva's mind.

However, Eva didn't have time for the fight-or-flight response to even kick in. In another quick motion, Paige sunk the blade of her knife into Eva's chest, just below her collarbone… and then a third time into the side of Eva's neck.

Paige then let Eva's body fall to the ground. Eva quickly lost consciousness as the pool of blood grew around her. Paige picked up Eva's suitcase and walked off into the night.

ᐧ ᐧ ᐧ ᐧ ᐧ ᐧ

The following morning Paige woke up to the sound of her

alarm clock with no recollection of the previous night's events. She began her morning routine and met Hayden for breakfast as planned.

"So, you're feeling okay?" Hayden asked her as they sat down at a table with their food.

"Yeah, I've been a little out of it recently, I will admit," she replied. "But this morning, I actually feel refreshed and ready to get this semester over with."

Hayden changed the subject, and the two caught up as they finished breakfast. He told Paige that Abby was planning a night out at a bar downtown that evening.

"Ask her about it when you see her in class," Hayden recommended since Paige and Abby were both in the class she was about to attend.

"Will do!" Paige told Hayden as she grabbed her bag and prepared to walk to class. "I'll probably take my own car and meet you all there since I have that early morning class tomorrow."

"Okay, see you there," Hayden replied and started walking in the opposite direction toward his own class.

Later that evening, Hayden arrived at the bar and quickly spotted Dan, Abby, Samantha, and Clark at a table near the billiards area. Dan raised a pitcher of beer to indicate that Hayden didn't need to buy a drink just yet. As Hayden sat down and poured his first glass of the night, Abby leaned over toward him.

"Did you see Paige at all this morning?" she asked.

"Yeah, we had breakfast together," Hayden replied. "Then she headed off to your guys' class."

"She didn't show up to class," Abby told Hayden.

"What?" Hayden said, not believing what he had heard. "She literally had her backpack and everything and was walking that way when she left breakfast."

"I'm going to try and call her," Abby advised and tried to ring Paige's cell phone.

Hayden and Abby gave each other concerned looks as the call went to voicemail. The rest of the group now joined the conversation.

"Maybe the breakfast hit her the wrong way, and she went home instead," Dan offered as a possible explanation.

"I guess it's possible," Hayden responded. "But you would think that she would send a text or something."

"She's kind of been blowing us all off lately," Clark added. "Maybe she's just stressed out and needs her space."

"You know what," Hayden replied, slightly exasperated. "I'll just go check on her in the morning. Let's all enjoy tonight. If she wants to be here, then she'll show up sooner or later."

طاقة

Chapter Three

Bloodlines

54,000 BC:

The sun rose over the hills near a small village somewhere in the Middle East. Within an hour of sunrise, the village was brimming with activity… children ran through the spaces in between dwellings, men began work on constructing a new housing unit for a family that had outgrown their current home, and several women journeyed down to a nearby riverbed to collect water for the villagers.

The tight-knit society worked together as a whole for the betterment of every member. Though every citizen was treated equally, the village had a small group that functioned as a leadership council. One of the members of this group was Ahjiamed, a tall thirty-six-year-old man with hair as dark as coal and brown eyes that often reflected the years of hard work he had dedicated to the service of his homeland. His physique bore the evidence of his labor in both muscle and a scattering of scars.

Ahjiamed was one of the men working on the new dwelling that morning. They attempted to get as much work done as possible before the heat of the midday sun forced them into a break. As the hours drew on, the group of men recessed from their building activities for a few hours. Ahjiamed walked over to the village's thriving agricultural area to visit his friend and fellow village leader, Koshili, who was hard at work tending to several crops. Ahjiamed watched as Koshili lifted his hands over his head, palms toward the rows of crops. The back of his right hand started to glow with the imprinted outline of a symbol that resembled ماء. Koshili pushed forward with his hands, seemingly against some invisible barrier, and torrents of water rushed outward from them, raining over the crops. After the field was adequately covered in water, Koshili lowered his hands to his sides, and the glowing symbol faded away.

"Hard at work still, my friend?" Ahjiamed remarked.

"As always," Koshili replied. "How is the building coming along?"

"We should be done by the end of the day, with plenty

of time for a dinner gathering," Ahjiamed said confidently.

The two men began walking down through the rows of crops so that Koshili could check on their condition. As they conversed, Ahjiamed's eyes wandered toward the sky, and he caught a glimpse of a bright flash just over the horizon.

"Did you see that, Koshili?" Ahjiamed asked his friend.

"No, I've been staring at this corn. What did you see?" Koshili replied.

"On the horizon, over there, a flash of light," Ahjiamed said as he pointed toward the abnormality.

The two men stood in their place, staring at the horizon for a few moments until they saw a trail of fire streaking across the sky. The trail emanated from the point on the horizon that Ahjiamed had seen the flash. As it approached, the fiery object flew over their heads before seemingly colliding with the ground about a half mile south of their location. The two men looked at each other in bewilderment for a moment before running back towards the central part of the village.

As they returned to the village, they found the other citizens in an uproar after seeing the fire trail cutting through the sky. Ahjiamed, Koshili and several other men from the village decided to head off in the direction that the object seemed to have made contact with the Earth.

As the group neared the end of the fiery trail, they

found a large crater in the ground, with the surrounding vegetation still burning. Ahjiamed and the others walked to the edge of the crater in an attempt to see if they could determine what made the large hole in the ground. Through the smoke, they eventually made out the shape of a figure. The unknown figure spotted their presence at the same time.

In an instant, the figure disappeared from the center of the crater and reappeared about fifteen feet in front of them. Ahjiamed and his companions immediately took a defensive stance. The figure before them stood about seven feet tall, bipedal, almost humanoid, but distinctly not. Its skin, if you could call it that, was more of an exterior shell of dull stone-like armor. The creature had a distinct orange glow emanating from its body. Ahjiamed poised his hands at his sides with his palms pointed to the ground. The symbol بَرْق appeared glowing on the back of his right hand, and electricity crackled from his palms. One of his companions also activated his powers, forming a protective barrier around the group by manipulating the earth's energy forces.

The creature spoke. "I am an Alva'ci, a visitor from another world. I have come to evaluate this planet for the use of my species."

"The use of your species?" Ahjiamed replied.

"Yes, the Alva'ci require new planets to survive, and

this planet has been identified as a possible host. I promise that your deaths will be quick and as painless as possible so that our greatly superior society may flourish."

"We will not let our world and our children die so that you can take our homes and erase our existence," Koshili insisted.

"You may fight if you desire, but I will defeat you. Then I will move onward to village after village, eliminating every last trace of your species from this planet," the Alva'ci responded.

Ahjiamed had seemingly heard enough of the invader's plans and directed the lightning crackling within his palms towards the Alva'ci. The creature absorbed the strike into a forcefield-like aura surrounding its body and redirected it back toward the group. The protective barrier around the group also absorbed the lightning, leaving them unharmed.

Ahjiamed kept the lightning crackling within his right palm and raised his left hand to the sky. The back of that hand illuminated with the symbol نار. Fire appeared to float above his left palm. Ahjiamed closed his eyes and concentrated on the Alva'ci in his thoughts. On the back of his right hand, another symbol appeared resembling خاطِر. The Alva'ci seemed to stumble, and Ahjiamed pushed his thoughts into the mind of the Alva'ci. Koshili seized the opportunity and activated his power, sending a torrent of water against the creature for a moment. Ahjiamed followed Koshili's attack by sending a pillar of electricity enshrouded in flames at the Alva'ci.

The Alva'ci fell to the ground. The group stood behind the protective barrier, cautious but hopeful that the threat had been eliminated. A few moments later, the Alva'ci rose back to its feet.

"Quite the effort… and honestly more than I thought was capable of such a fledgling civilization," the Alva'ci remarked. "I suppose you may put up an admirable fight, but in the end, the result will still be the same. The only thing that will change is the fact that I will now enjoy killing your people. As for the seven of you, I will wound and maim you, render you incapable of fighting, and then force you to watch as I slaughter your women and children… Make you listen to their screams as I tear their limbs from their bodies, cut deep into their flesh, and drain the life from them in front of you. I will laugh as I watch the light fade from your children's eyes as they beg and plead for mercy while I slowly crush their necks and leave them gasping for air."

Before Ahjiamed or any of the group could respond to the creature's threats, the Alva'ci vanished in a flash of orange light. The group instinctively looked back in the direction of their village to see an identical orange glow appear, quickly followed by a giant fireball rising upwards toward the sky. The group of men raced back towards their village, hoping they would arrive in time to save their loved ones.

Several minutes later, they found the Alva'ci making good on its threats as they arrived in the village. The creature was indiscriminately torturing and killing villagers. The bodies of men, women, and children were mangled and strewn about the roads. Ahjiamed, Koshili, and the others confronted the Alva'ci in the middle of the village. The creature stared at them with dark eyes and what seemed to be a look of enjoyment as it held a young woman in its fist. With the other hand, the Alva'ci dug a sharp claw-like nail into her side. The young woman screamed out in agonizing pain as the Alva'ci pulled its nail downward, carving a gaping hole in her side. As blood poured profusely from her wound, the creature tore a leg from her body as easily as one might pluck a feather from a bird and then tossed her flailing body aside to inevitably die.

Ahjiamed was infuriated and activated both his fire and electrical powers simultaneously, sending a barrage of energy at the Alva'ci. The creature deflected Ahjiamed's attack toward a nearby group of villagers, killing them instantly.

Several more villagers came running to Ahjiamed and the others to aid them in the fight.

"What can we do?" asked one of the young men that came running.

"Go and get Abbas," Ahjiamed responded to him. "The rest of you stay here and direct your powers at that creature. Protect the innocent."

The young man quickly returned with an older man. The group was putting up a fight but barely landing any significant blows against the Alva'ci. The older man, Abbas, came to Ahjiamed's side.

"Abbas, if we are going to have any chance of winning in this fight, we will need you to pour all of your strength out," Ahjiamed told him. "You must use all of your powers. You must use all seven spells at once."

"All seven spells?" asked Abbas, not quite believing yet that such measures were necessary.

"You have not seen the devastation that this creature has unleashed or what it is capable of. We will not have a chance without giving everything," Ahjiamed replied.

"I understand," said Abbas.

Abbas took a step back, closed his eyes, and raised his hands toward the sky. His voice changed, now deep and resounding. He spoke the words of the seven spells:

"Abarus,"

"Tithethus,"

"Emiratus,"

"Prophesch'naya Con'di Ashante,"

"Chantiatus,"

"Youlvasius,"

"Amal Esta Preavius."

With each utterance, the effects of that spell appeared instantaneously. First, a host of celestial beings appeared around the Alva'ci and engaged it in the battle. Secondly, threads of rope made of glowing light bound the Alva'ci by the arms, legs, and torso, restricting its ability to counter incoming attacks. With the third spell, the others in the group activated their powers, now amplified by the spell's effects, and cast them all at the Alva'ci. Next, a blanket of darkness fell over the Alva'ci, preventing it from seeing and clouding its thoughts. The fifth spell surrounded the group with a protective forcefield. The sixth spell increased the accuracy of each of the men's attacks, maximizing their effects and damage. The final spell opened dozens of energy portals around the group, multiplying the group's powers and sending a mirror of attacks at the Alva'ci through the portals from all angles.

Abbas held his position and kept the effects of the spells strong. After several minutes of the barrage of attacks, the Alva'ci fell to the ground. The group held their attacks steady even after the creature fell to ensure it was dead. As the group finally ceased their attacks, they cautiously approached the smoking body of the Alva'ci.

"Is it dead?" Koshili asked.

Abbas walked up to the Alva'ci to observe it.

"It appears that it is still alive," Abbas stated.

"There is no way that is possible," Ahjiamed exclaimed. "Nothing has ever survived such an attack!"

The body of the Alva'ci began to faintly glow with an orange light, and it began to move slightly.

"What can we do?" Koshili asked Abbas. "We cannot continue to fight this creature like this. It will eventually overpower all of us."

Abbas stood and contemplated the severity of the situation for a few moments before making a recommendation.

"After witnessing the power of this creature… as I see it, there is only one thing that we can possibly do if we hope to save humanity."

"What is that?" asked Ahjiamed.

"I can cast a spell, but I will need all of you to concentrate all of your powers on me while I do so. It will take everything we have to accomplish and come at a great cost… but I believe it will work," Abbas replied gravely.

"We must do whatever it takes," Ahjiamed stated matter-of-factly.

"Very well," Abbas replied. "Stand in a circle around me and be ready. I will cast protection on myself, and then I will amplify all of our powers again. Once I do that, I will need all of you to direct your powers at me as I cast the final spell."

The group was quiet as they moved into position around Abbas. The Alva'ci began to move again. This time it appeared as if it was almost strong enough to rise to its feet.

"Chantiatus," Abbas said, casting a spell of protection on himself.

"Emiratus," the group's powers now amplified to heightened levels.

Ahjiamed and the rest of the group activated their powers and cast them at Abbas in unison. As the Alva'ci started to shakily regain its composure and attempt to pull itself back up to a standing position, Abbas uttered:

"Nelitus Absoritum Malitus."

A blinding column of light tore through the sky and engulfed the Alva'ci. As the dust settled around the village, Ahjiamed cautiously walked over to where the Alva'ci had been slowly recovering. In its place was a cylindrical crater in the Earth's crust, ten feet in diameter and seemingly endless in depth.

"It appears that your plan worked!" Ahjiamed

exclaimed in fatigued relief.

"Yes, it would seem so," Abbas agreed, though his tone was less celebratory than it was plaintive. "What a bittersweet victory this is."

"You mentioned that this would come at a great cost. What is that cost?" Ahjiamed asked him.

As Abbas approached the others, the ground began to shake. The group watched as the massive hole in the Earth that the Alva'ci had vanished into collapsed in on itself, leaving nothing but a slight dimple in the ground to commemorate the battle.

"You will find that our lives will now become harder," Abbas finally announced when the earthquake subsided. "Try to use your powers, Ahjiamed."

As instructed, Ahjiamed raised a hand and attempted to summon one of his magical abilities. His posture changed as he discovered that he was unable to conjure any result. Ahjiamed strained in concentration as he attempted a second time. Abbas placed his hand on his friend's shoulder.

"The cost," Abbas muttered. "Our clan will have to return to the old ways of doing things… labor, agriculture, medicine, defense, everything. Just as before our sires gained the powers."

As the stark realization sunk in, a chorus of murmurs

and gasps spread throughout the small gathering of villagers. In a state of denial, various other villagers attempted to use their powers, all to no avail.

"Can't we simply undertake the same process that our fathers completed to regain what we have lost?" Ahjiamed asked as he looked around at the dismay spreading throughout the community.

"Unfortunately, we cannot," Abbas informed him. "The methods they used relied upon artifacts and entities that are no longer available to us."

"What about a'ltal bilv'at?" Ahjiamed suggested.

"That power is gone as well," Abbas told him solemnly. "We possess no means to regain any of the powers."

"Does that mean..?" Ahjiamed started.

"Our extended lifespans will fade, yes," Abbas had anticipated the question before Ahjiamed even brought it up. "You and I will likely live another fifty years. The next generation of our clan will possess normal lifespans."

Ahjiamed paced about the debris-ridden soil and ruminated over the upsetting news. He decided to use the nightly dinner gathering that evening to disperse the information to the remainder of the villagers.

ༀ ༀ ༀ ༀ ༀ ༀ

TWO YEARS LATER

Abbas sat at the table in his dwelling next to the dim light of a candle. His wife and children were still soundly asleep. He had woken suddenly in the middle of the night with his dream ingrained into his mind. As he recalled the vision, he wrote it down on parchment.

He had been standing in a dark, empty clearing devoid of others. He recollected that he had felt no desire to explore or even move. A voice called out to him as he stood silently in the expanse of the void. An unseen orator told Abbas that the powers his clan had lost in their battle with the Alva'ci still existed, though they were dormant. It explained that these remnants of their powers existed to keep the effects of Abbas' spell intact and keep the Alva'ci trapped under the Earth in a comatose state.

"What about when we die?" Abbas had called out to the voice, his query echoing in the vast darkness.

Once again, the unknown voice spelled out the future. It told Abbas that the remnants of their powers would pass on to new holders as the current ones perished. After the voice concluded its elucidation of the remnants of power, it narrated several lines that Abbas wrote down verbatim. He would later entitle those passages as The Parisifian Prophecy. This would be the first of several prophecies and visions that Abbas recorded before his eventual death.

AGENTS OF FATE

ضوء

Chapter Four

The Parisifian Prophecy

*"An eternal power subdued in flesh and bone.
Coming to light in a perilous world.
Among them stands a cognizant one, with whom fate is vested…
causing life and love to be lost or won."*

Hayden awoke to the trilling sounds of his alarm, slowly opening his eyes to the sliver of light streaming into his bedroom from between the curtains. As he made his way to the bathroom to turn on the shower, he flicked on the television. Hayden began to shave his face while the sounds of a news reporter's voice filled the bedroom with background noise.

"…out in New Braunfels, Texas, where a magnitude 6.8 earthquake just rocked the area. Geologists say that the quake originated from a long-inactive fault known as the Balcones Fault, which hasn't seen activity in several million years. Local resident Susan Knowles describes her experience…"

As Hayden stepped in to the steaming shower, the water washed over his head and drowned out the sounds from the television. While he lathered himself with soap, his thoughts inevitably focused on the fact that he hadn't heard from Paige in two days, and she hadn't been attending any of her classes. Her parents had already taken the steps to report her missing with the local police department, and they spoke to Hayden regularly with any updates.

Hayden dressed and grabbed a banana as he headed out the front door, forcing himself to still go to class instead of dwelling on his inability to find Paige. As he walked through the front doors of University Hall and made his way toward the elevators, his phone chirped with a text message notification.

Hayden grabbed his phone from his pocket and looked at the screen. He did a double-take once he read the notification to make sure that he wasn't seeing things… a text from Paige. He opened the messages app.

"In San Diego… Needed to clear my head. Be back in town tonight. Let's all catch a movie?" the text message read.

Hayden quickly typed a response. "Uhh yeah, sure. You okay? Call your parents. They legit reported you missing."

He then fired off another text to the large group message chain that he had going with friends and Paige's family to let them all know she had just texted him. The message thread immediately exploded into a series of questions and expressions of relief. Hayden tried to keep up with responses as he exited the elevator and walked down the hallway toward his classroom, now wondering if he should just skip class. After a few moments of thought, he decided to go since this class was only forty-five minutes long, and now he knew that everything was going to be okay.

The next forty-five minutes dragged on for what seemed like hours. Hayden was sure he would retain exactly zero knowledge from that particular class. He made his way across campus to the student union to meet up with Dan and Abby, checking his phone as he walked through the bustling quad. One more text message from Paige had come through while he was in class. It read, "I'm okay, better now. Wanna all meet at like 8:00 at the theater?"

Hayden finished reading the text just as he arrived at the table where Dan and Abby were eating lunch. Dan motioned to Hayden to sit down as he finished chewing the bite of sandwich he had just taken.

Hayden took a seat, and Dan immediately inquired. "Sooooo..? What happened?"

"I don't know," replied Hayden. "Paige randomly texted and said she left town down to SD to clear her head and that she's okay... She wants us all to meet up at eight o'clock to catch a movie."

"Weird," was the only response that Dan could come up with.

"Yeah, you're telling me. No contact for two days, and now she wants to watch a movie…" replied Hayden.

Abby chimed in. "Maybe she just had a lot to process, and now she wants to spend some stress-free time relaxing with the people she feels safe with."

"I guess so," Dan replied. "It still seems weird to me. She like never misses a class, and if something is bothering her, she always lets one of us know."

"Well, let's just do the movie thing and chill… then once we get out of there, we can ask her about the specifics," Hayden added.

Dan and Abby nodded in agreement to the plan. The three of them got up and headed back to Abby's apartment to kill some time before Clark and Samantha were able to join them.

೮೨ ೮೨ ೮೨ ೮೨ ೮೨ ೮೨

Armond gazed into the mirror, examining his own face almost as if he had never seen himself before. Water dripped from his chin after the facial-cleanser commercial style splash he had just given himself. The clouded thoughts in his mind began to dissipate as he continued to stare at his reflection. As Armond finally snapped back to reality, he suddenly felt awakened with a purpose. He exited the bathroom and returned to the front of the bookstore he owned with his younger brother, Ahsan.

"Brother, I need you to run things around here for a while. I have to take a short trip and complete a task," Armond said to Ahsan as he arrived at the front desk.

"A trip? What task?" Ahsan replied, confused by the sudden request.

"It is a task that our father asked me to complete if I was ever called to do so. I won't be away too long."

"Father died eight years ago, Armond. What task did he ask of you?"

"A task that is handed down to the firstborn in every generation of our family. I cannot say more until I return… but trust me, I will tell you all about it then."

Ahsan sighed and shook his head in affirmation to Armond. As Armond grabbed his coat, car keys, and a box containing several old books, Ahsan joked. "Oh, and when you get back, I'm definitely taking my own vacation!"

"Of course, little brother," Armond replied, smirking at Ahsan. "Farewell. I should be back in about a week."

Ahsan waved as his brother exited the bookstore, the

bell on the front door ringing to mark his departure.

Armond tossed his coat on the passenger seat of his car and pulled away, heading toward LaGuardia airport. As he neared the airport, he mulled over the things that his father had taught him as an adolescent... the tale of a dark power and its eventual rise, the tale of powers handed down through the generations, the tale of his ancestors and their commitment to aiding those chosen to receive the powers, and the tale of the cognizant one and his mission to defeat the dark power. Armond had wondered when he was younger if these stories were simply that... stories. However, his father had instructed him that they were authentic. Armond's father had been told them by his father. The tales had been handed down to the firstborns of the family for as long as any of them had known.

Armond had, in all honesty, mostly forgotten about the tales until this morning when they came rushing back to his mind while standing in front of that mirror. Along with these memories came what Armond could only describe to himself as a moment of divine instruction... and, in listening to that instruction, he arrived and parked at LaGuardia, then boarded a plane for John Wayne Airport in Santa Ana, California. Shortly after taking his seat, the pilot came on over the intercom system and announced that the weather on the way looked great and their flight should arrive at 7:14 p.m. Pacific Time.

૭૭ ૭૭ ૭૭ ૭૭ ૭૭ ૭૭

Hayden, Dan, Abby, Samantha, and Clark gathered outside the movie theater in Brea Downtown. Paige still had not arrived. After a few minutes of waiting outside, Hayden texted Paige and told her that the group would go inside and get some snacks and seats and that she could just meet up with them in the theater.

Paige watched the group from inside a shop on the other side of the street. She waited for another text from Hayden, letting her know that they had sat down in the theater and where she could find them. Paige gave it ten more minutes before proceeding into the movie theater. As she walked down the hallway, she clutched at the dagger concealed underneath her jacket… the dagger she had used just several hours ago to slice through a young woman's neck in the town of Cataviña in Baja, California, Mexico. Shortly after that killing, the darkness inside Paige identified Hayden as the next target.

As Paige entered the actual theater, she quickly spotted the group of her friends sitting in the sixth row back. The lights had already dimmed, and movie trailers were playing on the screen. She discreetly made her way to the theater's back row and sat there for a few minutes observing Hayden and the others.

Near the end of the final trailer, Paige rose from her seat and slowly made her way to the row behind her group of friends. As the trailer ended and the light level in the theater was almost nonexistent, Paige drew the dagger from inside her coat and readied herself.

Hayden suddenly felt that all too familiar feeling that he had been dealing with all his life, though this time, it was stronger. His vision blurred, and an intense chill ran down his spine. However, this time, the feeling was accompanied by a fleeting image that entered his mind that caused him to subconsciously jump up out of his seat.

A fraction of a second later, Paige's dagger ripped through the metal backing and the cushion of Hayden's seat. Hayden looked back in awe and disbelief as he first saw the blade fixed in the place where his chest had just been moments earlier and then saw Paige's expressionless face staring at him.

Paige reached down for the hilt of the dagger as if she was going to withdraw it from the seat and continue her attack. Hayden felt a sudden rush throughout his body, like an intense heat emanating from his core. Out of nowhere, the back of his right hand began to glow with the symbol ضوء. Paige observed this and more fervently pulled at the dagger so that she could finish the act. Hayden instinctively raised his palms facing toward the theater's ceiling, and a blinding pure white light filled the room. After a few seconds, the light dissipated, and everyone's sight began to adjust back… Paige was nowhere to be found.

Dan, Samantha, Abby, and Clark all leapt from their seats and screamed in panic at what had just occurred. As they clamored about the aisle in fear and disbelief, attempting to figure out what to do, Hayden continued to stand in the same position… still in shock that Paige, of all people, had just tried to murder him. A few moments later, Dan shook Hayden to snap him out of his daze.

"Hayden! Buddy, are you with me? What in the hell just happened? Was that really Paige?" Dan fired off a round of confused and worried questions.

"Yeah…" Hayden simply replied, taking a few moments before continuing. "We should get out of here."

"I agree. We need to go call the cops or something. This is just unbelievable," Dan added.

The group of friends made their way out of the theater and into the lobby, where crowds of people were still in line for tickets and concessions as if nothing unusual had happened. Hayden and his friends emerged through the front doors of the building into the courtyard. Hayden took a deep breath of the slightly chilled evening air and felt some semblance of normality returning to his body.

As Hayden breathed out and opened his eyes, he was startled to find a man that appeared to be running toward him and the group.

"Hayden!" the unfamiliar man called out as he continued to run in their direction.

"Do you know that guy?" Dan asked Hayden, confused.

"No… I don't," Hayden replied with a tinge of worry in his voice after what had just occurred inside the theater.

The man stopped running about fifteen feet in front of the group of friends and caught his breath.

"Hayden, right?" the man asked.

"Umm, yeah, that's me. Who are you?" Hayden replied cautiously.

"My name is Armond. I got here as quickly as I could. Something just happened to you, right? Someone tried to kill you?" the man explained.

"How… did you… know that?" Hayden questioned.

"Let me explain. Can we go somewhere more private

to talk? Your friends can come along if you'd like," Armond replied.

"Okay, this is weird. I mean, okay, yeah, there's a coffee shop around the corner with some booths in the back," Hayden agreed, though stumbling over his words.

"I'll come with you, man," Dan said.

"Do you mind if I take the girls home? We're all kind of shaken up?" Clark asked Hayden, motioning to Abby and Samantha.

"Yeah, and as much as I'd love to stay and hear all this, I should probably go study for my 'Algo' Engineering class," Abby interjected, referencing one of her upcoming computer science course finals.

"Yeah, of course, you guys go. Clark, get them back home safe, please," Hayden responded.

Clark, Abby, and Samantha walked off toward the parking garage while Hayden and Dan accompanied Armond on the short walk to the coffee shop. As they arrived inside, Hayden waved at the manager and asked if they could get "the usual" brought to their booth in the rear of the building. The manager waved back and gave Hayden a thumbs up.

The three walked down a short hallway into a room with two large booths. The room was empty, and they took a seat in the booth that Hayden and his group of friends frequented fairly regularly.

"Okay, so who exactly are you, and what's going on?" Hayden began the conversation.

"My name is Armond. I own a bookstore in New York with my brother. That's not important, though," Armond replied. "My family has a kind of tradition… a tale of responsibility that is passed down from generation to generation."

Hayden and Dan listened to Armond's story with interest, and the shop manager arrived at their booth with three drinks and a plate full of bite-size sandwiches. Hayden thanked the manager and let him know he'd handle the bill on the way out.

Armond continued. "The story that is passed down tells of an event that happened in the middle east just over 56,000 years ago. A creature, not of this world, arrived and attempted to destroy all of humanity to make way for the remaining members of its species."

Hayden and Dan's interest was now piqued. Armond took a drink of his coffee and continued.

"This creature almost succeeded. Many people were injured or died in the village that it landed near. After every measure they took, the creature was still alive and beginning to rise back up to continue its slaughter."

"Sorry…" Hayden interjected. "What exactly does

this story have to do with me and my friends being attacked?"

"You. You were being attacked, Hayden. Your friends weren't ever the target," Armond replied.

"Okay. So why?" Hayden inquired again.

"The people in that village all those years ago had a characteristic that you'll find very much in common with you," Armond explained. "call it magic, I suppose... or powers."

Hayden interrupted... "Magic?"

"You experienced something in the theater, didn't you? Some kind of unexplainable event and a feeling that overwhelmed your senses," Armond queried. "I felt it when the power activated."

"Uhhh... yeah," Hayden shakily replied. "I had this feeling happen that I've always had since I was a kid... then all of a sudden, I had like this hazy image of a dagger flash through my mind real quick that made me jump out of my seat right before my... friend... tried to kill me."

"And then?" Armond urged Hayden to continue.

"Then it felt like this fire growing inside me... one of my hands, it started glowing on the backside, some strange symbol or letter or something..." Hayden replied. "Then there was this blinding white light. Once I could see again, Paige was gone."

"Paige is the girl that tried to kill him," Dan offered in explanation.

Hayden continued. "Yeah, Paige is one of my best friends. She has been acting really strange lately. She disappeared for a few days, and we were all meeting tonight after she finally came back on the grid."

"Hayden, Dan… I hate to tell you this, but that is not Paige," Armond said as he looked at the two. "At least not the Paige that you know."

"What do you mean?" Dan asked.

"The creature that came to Earth all those years ago… Well, those villagers used their powers to try and defeat it. Powers like the one that you experienced, Hayden, and many more powers. Even then, they still almost lost. Ultimately, they came together and cast a powerful spell using everything they had. It disabled the creature into a comatose-like state and buried it far underground. In the process, though, everyone on Earth that had these powers lost them."

Armond took another drink of his coffee before continuing. Hayden and Dan took a moment to sip on theirs as well.

"After that moment, though the use of these powers had been eliminated from everyday life, they continued to exist in a dormant state. Ten people were chosen to possess these remnants of power to keep the creature unable to rise again. As these people passed away, their power was randomly transferred to another person. The power usually went to an infant or child… and it has continued to pass down through the generations of humanity. Every so often, all throughout the lives of the ten chosen ones, these benign powers would activate, and together those powers would renew the spell on the creature, keeping it comatose. The activation of those powers, to the person, feels like an intense chill running down their spine."

"Okay, I didn't tell you what that feeling felt like before…" Hayden said as he pondered. "Usually, it like blurs my vision also, and I almost feel like something emanating from me, if that makes sense."

"Have you ever experienced any of these powers, like the light, before in your life?" Armond asked.

"Ummm… I don't think so," Hayden replied, looking off toward the ceiling as if in thought. "I mean, I've had dreams before… like a dream just recently of someone that looked strikingly similar to Paige killing some guy in a strange city. That was right before she went on vacation with her family to Yosemite."

"A dream… Ane'illuminus, perhaps," Armond mused.

"What?" Hayden asked as he popped a bite-size

sandwich in his mouth.

"Ane'illuminus is one of the ancient powers," Armond continued.

"Wait, I thought like the real powers were gone, though, you said?" Dan interjected.

"Yes..." Armond stumbled on his words before proceeding. "They are gone... or were gone... The reason that ten people were chosen to hold the remnants of the powers was that a minimum of six different individual life forces were necessary to keep the spell intact. Ten were chosen as kind of a..."

"Failsafe?" Hayden inquisitively finished Armond's sentence.

"Exactly. If, for example, three of these ten people somehow died in an extremely short period of time, then there were still several others that possessed the powers until three more people inherited the powers of the deceased."

"Okay, but that doesn't explain why I seem to be getting real powers," Hayden said to Armond.

"No, it doesn't," Armond agreed. "The remnants pass on to a new person usually within a day. The actual powers wouldn't ever manifest in individuals again unless something was disrupting that."

"So, what would disrupt that?" Hayden asked.

"To answer that simply… You," Armond replied.

"Wait, me?" Hayden followed up in disbelief. "How am I doing this?"

"We're getting off on tangents," Armond explained. "Let me continue the story; it should answer all these questions."

Hayden nodded in agreement.

Armond continued. "Along with the ten holders of these remnants of the powers, a man named Abbas was chosen to act as a sort-of watcher and keeper of the lore. This responsibility was passed down through his descendants, eventually reaching me. Our family has none of the remnants of the powers, but we can feel the presence of the ten and sometimes communicate with them telepathically. This ability has never manifested in all of my family's generations until now."

Hayden and Dan listened intently. The coffee shop manager returned to the booth, provided the three with more drinks, and then departed.

Armond picked up again. "Abbas had several visions and prophecies of future events. One of these was called the Parisifian Prophecy. It tells of an unknown time in the future in which one individual that holds remnants of the powers would be known as the 'cognizant one.' They would have a feeling since childhood that they were… special, for lack of a better word. Their actual power would manifest itself in a limited fashion beginning in their childhood. Does that sound at all like you, Hayden?"

"I mean, yeah… I've kind of always felt like that, I suppose. But I guess I just thought it was me being a stupid kid and like dreaming big or whatever," Hayden replied. "I guess I've had lots of dreams that ended up coming true, but they were just dumb little things, nothing serious. Just like some silly deja vu feeling stuff."

"Well, it's much more than that," Armond countered. "According to the prophecy, at some point in the cognizant one's life, some of the other ten will begin to die… but instead of the remnants of power passing to other individuals to keep a balance, the powers will transfer to the cognizant one creating an imbalance. Once a fifth remnant holder dies, the effects of the spell keeping the creature comatose will weaken to the point that it is able to break free. Then, we're looking at either extinction or the ability of the remaining power-holders to finally kill this creature once and for all."

"So, again, how does Paige factor into all of this?" Dan asked.

"I believe," Armond answered. "That somehow the essence of the creature was able to find a weak point in the Earth's mantle and crust… and while even in a comatose-like state, a part of its power was able to corrupt someone, specifically your friend Paige. You said that she recently went on vacation with her family?"

"Yeah, to Yosemite National Park. Not very long ago at all," Hayden replied.

"It must have been there then," Armond continued. "The creature likely would have taken control of her body and mind in order to eliminate the remnant holders and force its re-emergence. Has she seemed different since she came back?"

Dan immediately answered. "Yeah, like right after she got back, we went to dinner, and she disappeared for the whole night. When I went over to her apartment the next day to see if she was there, she was completely out of it, all scratched up and bruised, and she had no idea where she had been."

Hayden reluctantly nodded his head in agreement with Dan's analysis, fearing what this meant for Paige.

"I'm sorry to say," Armond replied. "But Paige was likely killed or corrupted by this creature while she was out there on vacation. She probably came upon a cavern or cave of some sort that the creature had identified as the weak spot I mentioned. Her not remembering entire nights makes me think that this creature is controlling her... using her mind to mimic her normal personality and characteristics. Then in the times that she blacks out, the creature is acting on its own will to murder those with the remnants of the powers."

"Fuck," Dan said in a somber tone, with his head down.

"How do we know this, though?" Hayden asked.

"You're going to have to go there, Hayden," Armond replied. "Go to the spot she went with her family. You'll have to find the location and see for yourself if this is true."

"Okay," was all that Hayden could manage to say.

"If it is true, Hayden… if you do find this spot… you should fully expect to be attacked. Most likely by Paige again. You'll have to remember that it isn't actually Paige controlling her body. If she kills you, Hayden, then we're all likely dead in a matter of days."

Hayden sat in silence and pondered everything Armond had just told them. On any other day, Hayden would have laughed the man off as crazy, but unfortunately, this all made sense today.

"Okay, let's do this," Hayden replied.

Armond nodded at him and Dan. The three of them discussed specific strategies while finishing up the plate of mini-sandwiches and their drinks. At the conclusion of the meal, Hayden paid the store manager, and the group walked out onto the still bustling downtown sidewalks.

———

Hayden led Armond and Dan into his apartment and closed the front door behind them. Armond suggested that they use the backyard for Hayden to attempt to summon his powers, and the trio gathered there.

"So far, we know you have the acquired power of Light and then your own inherent power of Ane'illuminus," Armond told Hayden. "Now let's figure out which other ones you have acquired."

"Okay, how do we do that?" Hayden asked. "I've never actually voluntarily used these powers."

"Close your eyes and concentrate," Armond told him. "Focus on finding the powers within yourself. You will feel them activating. When you do, just let the power sit there on the cusp, and we should see the symbols of what you have acquired glow on the back of your hands."

Hayden followed Armond's instructions and closed his eyes. He searched for that feeling he had felt last time one of the powers activated on its own. After a few minutes of intense concentration, Armond and Dan noticed a faint glow coming from the back of Hayden's right hand.

"Dude, you're doing it!" Dan exclaimed.

Hayden opened his eyes and looked at his hand. He

continued to focus on the feeling of power that was starting to rise within him. The symbol began to glow brighter.

"That's Fire," Armond told him. "Point your hand towards that piece of wood and let the power rise up."

Within seconds of obeying Armond's direction, Hayden's hand flowed with a beam of fire. The fire ignited the piece of wood in an instant. Armond quickly grabbed the garden hose and put the fire out.

"That was great," Armond congratulated him. "Now remember that feeling for Fire, and you will be able to summon that power in the future when you want to."

"Let's do another," Hayden said, now excited that he was able to summon these powers at will.

The three of them stayed up until 4:00 a.m. practicing Hayden's newfound powers. They discovered that he possessed the powers of Light, Electricity, and Energy Manipulation, in addition to Fire and Ane'illuminus.

⋅ ⋅ ⋅ ⋅ ⋅ ⋅

The following day and night went by as a blur, with Dan and Armond staying at Hayden's apartment and using the time to refine his use of the powers. On Sunday morning, Armond was confident that Hayden was ready to confront Paige.

"You're sure that I'm ready?" Hayden asked Armond as he packed a bag to leave for Yosemite.

"I'm sure," Armond reassured him. "Your powers will enhance your senses to enable you to find the location where the Alva'ci corrupted Paige. Once you find the spot, be very aware and cautious. I expect the Alva'ci to try to trick you and use your friendship with Paige against you. Be ready for anything."

Hayden nodded his head in acknowledgment. He said goodbye to Dan and Armond and headed out the door.

"I hope this goes well," Dan said to Armond.

"As do I," Armond said in agreement. "Take care of yourself, Dan. I am going to contact my brother and then find a place to rent here in town. I have a feeling I will be here longer than just a week. Please let me know if you hear from Hayden."

"Will do," Dan replied, and the two left the apartment.

℃ ℃ ℃ ℃ ℃ ℃

Six hours later, Hayden arrived at Yosemite National Park. After parking his car, he scrolled through Paige's Instagram feed to see if he could recognize any of the pictures she had posted on the day she had arrived at the park with her parents. He spotted one that looked familiar and headed in that direction.

Arriving at the campsite that Paige had stayed at, Hayden looked around and contemplated where she might have gone after that. He closed his eyes and tried to focus on letting his powers guide him in the right direction. After scanning the surrounding area, Hayden set off towards an area of forest surrounding a nearby mountain that felt right to him.

As Hayden explored the area near the foothills of the mountain, he caught a glimpse of something peculiar in his peripheral vision. Hayden wandered closer and discovered a small entrance in the mountainside that looked as if time and all humankind had forgotten it. He squeezed through and found himself inside a dark cave.

As Hayden looked around, he noticed the glistening of the rocks on the walls of the cave. They gave off a faint orangish glow that seemed to fade and grow in intensity. He ran his hand along the smooth stone slab in the middle of the cave. It was cold to the touch.

"You made it," a familiar feminine voice said from behind him.

Hayden quickly turned around to see Paige standing near the entrance to the cave. The rocks on the wall seemed to glow brighter.

"Paige," Hayden started. "Listen, if there's any part of you left in there, I can help you defeat this thing and get you back home. We miss you."

"You fool," Paige responded coldly. "You cannot bring her back. Her body is mine, and I use it to manipulate your feeble kind so that I can end your existence. She is nothing more than a tool for me. Before you arrived, I expelled what is left of her soul from this body. It now lingers in this cave where it will remain in a state of constant torment until I vacate her flesh."

"In other words, until I kill you," Hayden responded.

"Highly unlikely," Paige replied as she walked over to the wall of the cave and snapped off jagged pieces of the orange rock in both her hands.

Paige ran towards Hayden, leaping over the slab in the middle of the room and thrusting at him with the dagger-like rocks. Hayden rolled out of the way to dodge the attack and then quickly rose back to his feet, stepping back to increase the distance between him and Paige.

"Just accept your death already," Paige taunted. "The sooner I kill you, the sooner I am able to rise again and conquer this planet."

Hayden held out his right hand in front of him and pointed it at Paige. The symbol of electricity lit brightly on the back of his hand, and a bolt of lightning streamed from it. Paige crossed the two pieces of orange rock in front of her as the stream of lightning approached her, deflecting the blast onto the stone slab.

"I see you figured out some of your powers," Paige mocked before once again running towards Hayden to attack.

Paige and Hayden exchanged several unsuccessful volleys of attacks at one another, seemingly coming to a stalemate. Hayden could see the impatience and scorn on Paige's face as she paced across the cave from him. He told himself that he only needed to stay alive and land one blow.

"I'm getting tired of these games," Paige said menacingly as she walked toward the center of the cave.

Hayden waited for Paige to resume attacking, trying to predict her next move. Paige approached the stone slab and placed her hand on top of it. Moments later, the ground within the cave began to violently shake. Hayden dove out of the way as several boulders fell from the roof of the cave toward him.

As Hayden regained his composure and attempted to stand back up, he saw Paige standing above him. He tried to spring back up, but Paige knelt down and thrust one of the jagged pieces of orange rock into his abdomen. Hayden cried out in excruciating pain as the rock sliced through his flesh.

Paige drew the second piece of rock in her other hand up and grasped it with both hands. She began to thrust it downward towards Hayden to strike a fatal blow. Hayden's survival instinct kicked in with an enormous rush of adrenaline. He raised both of his hands toward Paige's chest. Hayden watched in momentary disbelief as the back of both his hands lit up. Paige dropped the piece of jagged rock on the cave floor as intense streams of lightning and fire erupted from Hayden's hands and struck her in the chest. Paige's body flew backward against the stone slab, and she lay there motionless.

Hayden struggled to his feet, examining his side where Paige had stabbed him. Although he could see the shard of rock under his skin, he was surprised to find that the wound was sealed up and there was no blood. The pain seemed to have subsided as well. He walked over to the quiet body of Paige. The fire and lightning seemed to have effectively ended the fight. He knelt beside Paige's body and began to cry while holding her hand.

Several minutes later, Hayden gathered himself and decided that it was time to leave. He walked over to the wall of the cave where he had left his backpack when he'd entered. Returning to Paige's body, he opened the backpack and removed a spare shirt and pair of shorts that he had brought. The effects of the fire had decimated Paige's clothing to nothing more than ash, though her body remained unburned and unblemished other than a small scar below her left breast.

Hayden placed his spare clothes on Paige's nude body and then picked her up in his arms. As he exited the cave, Hayden let out a long sigh as he thought about what would come when he arrived home.

From behind him, Hayden heard a sound from inside the cave. As he turned around to examine the entrance, a light gust of wind flowed out of the cave and surrounded Hayden. The breeze swelled around him before it ascended upwards, shaking tree branches as it passed. Paige's pale features became flush with color once again. Hayden smiled as he realized his friend was now finally at peace.

Hayden carried Paige's body back to his car, which he had luckily parked in a relatively deserted area. He placed her in the rear seat and set off for Fullerton. When Hayden was within an hour of arriving, he called Dan to let him know everything that had happened and give him his ETA. Dan coordinated with Armond, and the three of them traveled together to Paige's parents' home in the morning to break the news and mourn together.

Over the next few days, Hayden, Dan, and Abby assisted the Hendersons with making funeral arrangements for their friend. As Hayden quietly sifted through stacks of photographs and papers, he happened upon a copy of the funeral program. He was only paying half attention as he browsed through it until his eyes spotted a name that gave him pause. Hayden had been so busy helping with preparations and comforting his friends that he somehow completely forgot about… her.

AGENTS OF FATE

جو

Chapter Five

The Fear of Falling Apart

Although the coffin of his best friend rested on the church stage a mere fifty feet in front of him, Hayden couldn't help but think of the inevitable moment that was coming. Any time now, the girl of his dreams was going to come walking through that door. He felt both horrible for it, as well as overcome with nervousness and delight. His best friend was dead. The girl that he loved, her sister, would finally return after two years of deafening silence and self-imposed isolation.

Kali. She had run away from the situation, shunning her plans and her people. For years, a subtle attraction had been there between her and Hayden. It grew between them, silently at first and then more blatant. They flirted; it seemed to Hayden that they were meant for each other. Their interests in common were numerous. Their attraction was undeniable, and they admitted it to each other countless times. However, just when things seemed to be going all right between them, Kali randomly chose to attend college in the Northwest instead of Orange County as she had planned... It was all out of nowhere.

A day before leaving, she briefly explained to Hayden that she felt like if she stuck around, the relationships between her, Hayden, and Paige would suffer... so she had to leave. The next day she was gone. It was wholly unsatisfactory. Hayden called Kali several times afterward, to no response. He eventually resigned, accepting that maybe sometimes things just weren't meant to be... but he never really believed it deep down. He knew that they were connected, but he gave in to the idea that he needed to move on. Weakness, maybe... or perhaps just giving her the space she needed. Bullshit is what it was. She had copped out, in his mind. She ran away instead of standing up for what she wanted, what they both knew they wanted.

But now... she was finally coming back. Under the most unfortunate of circumstances, of course. That was Hayden's cruel sense of luck, it seemed. It was hardly an opportune moment to rekindle a lost romance, so he sat there in the church pew, reflecting on the girl that was his best friend.

Tragedy had befallen her just over two weeks prior, yet he had seen her just a few days ago. Given that she had literally tried to kill him at that time... however, that wasn't really her, but a shadow of her possessed by an evil that no one fully comprehended yet.

Then she walked into the church. Kali. She wore a black dress, of course, yet it complimented her figure so gracefully. She was as beautiful as ever. Hayden couldn't help but look, perhaps stare at her as she entered the room. His all-too-long gaze was returned by Kali. It was like they sought out each other's eyes... of course, they did. This awkward moment had been years in the making. The occurrence was inevitable. She took a seat next to her parents in the row just in front of him. Hayden rose from his seat and walked up to them, paying his condolences and hugging each of them. As he came to Kali, he paused. They both said their obligatory "I'm sorry" in unison. The hug was filled with warmth, awkwardness, and maybe... just maybe a hint of regret. Definitely regret on Hayden's part, he thought. Maybe he should have tried harder. But it almost seemed to him that there was regret on Kali's part also... that she had all but shunned him for the most asinine of reasons. After all, Hayden thought, it's not like Paige would have disapproved. She had admittedly noticed the attraction between Hayden and Kali and all but gave it her blessing. But Kali refused to let that be enough. She was convinced that it would drive a wedge between two or all of them. So she ran away. That sat heavily on Hayden's mind. If Kali was that ready to give up so easily, was there really a future between them?

The hug ended. Yes, it definitely lasted longer than those with her parents. Hayden couldn't help but mull the possible meaning of it over and over in his mind. He excused himself and took his seat in the pew immediately behind Kali. The pastor walked to his place at the lectern on stage and spoke into the microphone, asking everyone to take their seats. Thus began one of the saddest days of Hayden's memory, yet one filled with the potential to repair bridges that he longed so much to finally have the chance to cross.

Halfway through the service, a pain started growing in Hayden's side where Paige had stabbed him with the shard of orange rock. As the pain became more intense, Hayden noticed what seemed to be a faint glow of orange from under his shirt. He pulled his jacket over his side to hide it. His hands felt warmer, and then the feeling hit again. His vision blurred, and an intense chill ran down his spine. As it passed, Hayden noticed again the warmth in his hands growing. A small flame ignited in the middle of his right palm.

"Not now," he thought.

He had almost managed to forget these powers for the day. He quickly clasped his hands shut, putting out the flame. The faint clap of his hands prompted Kali to look back in his direction. Hayden gave her a look and smile that was meant to convey something like "Oops and sorry." She smiled back at him and returned her attention to the pastor. The chill faded, as did the flame. Hayden continued to alternate his attention between the pastor's words and the girl that he still loved so intently. After all, what could the pastor say that he couldn't say a thousand times better? He knew Paige so much better than anyone. Would she forgive him for splitting his attention between this service and her sister? He thought she would… She knew that he loved Kali. After she had left, Paige and Hayden had discussed it in depth.

"Even Kali knew the potential that was there between them," Hayden thought to himself. She had acknowledged it on dozens of occasions. She just refused to let it be what it could be. Hayden sat there, staring at the back of her head as he zoned out, thinking of all the times that they had spent together. All of the concerts, the plays, the nights of music and singing, the unplanned cuddling and spending the night on the couch together. It was all a confusing mixture of feelings… love, betrayal, nervousness, and angst.

"What the hell was her problem? Her hangup?"

Hayden thought. "This needs a resolution."

The pastor concluded his remarks, and the service ended. Everyone in attendance made their rounds, speaking to each other about Paige and offering their condolences. Once again, Hayden met Kali face to face.

"It's been quite a while…" was all Hayden could muster to say… like a complete idiot, he thought to himself.

"Yeah, I'm sorry for that," Kali replied. "I was really confused. Obviously, this doesn't really help things… for either of us, I'm sure… but I just want you to know that I've been thinking about everything, about us, ever since I left."

"Really?" Hayden questioned. In his mind, she had all but forgotten him.

"Yes, of course… I can't just forget what was there. I'm not going to deny that we had something, but you know that I was conflicted about what to do. Maybe it seemed to you like I chose the easy way out, but at the time, that was the path I took. I can't explain why, but you know what I told you."

Hayden knew what she said at the time… it was burned in his memory. Yes, it was, to him, the easy way out. He thought she was afraid of what could be between the two of them. Over the years, they had grown to love each other in many different ways, as friends and even in an almost sibling-like way. However, over the years, that gave way to a romantic interest. They both realized the immense connection they had.

It started innocently enough. Hayden recalled the time that they flew out to Boston together to visit Paige. She was working on an internship in the city. They all stayed in her company-paid rental home in Newton, about twenty minutes outside the city. Hayden and Kali spent the majority of every day with each other for those three weeks… and it was then that they really started to notice they had feelings for each other. After some time of dancing around the obvious, they began to go out together and interact as a couple. To Hayden, at least, it confirmed everything he felt. He could tell that Kali felt it too.

But then she left. She left Hayden feeling betrayed like she had punched him as hard as she could in the stomach… taking his breath away. For the past couple of years, he agonized over it. As much as he tried to move on and forget her, he still felt the connection deep down.

"Yeah, I know what you said, Kali… but for what it's worth, I thought it was bullshit then, and I still do. I don't mean to be an asshole, and I'm not trying to come off like that… but we had something real. You know it, and so do I. Every time that I saw you, whenever you walked into the room, I felt what was between us. I wasn't the one to just let go."

"I know... I need to think, Hayden," Kali responded. "I mean, I've been thinking about it all this time, don't get me wrong. Don't act like I didn't love you because I did. I just didn't want to screw things up between everyone."

"You wouldn't have though..." Hayden returned argumentatively. "If you'd have listened to your sister instead of running away, you would have known that... Nevermind, I don't want to argue, and I don't want to disrespect Paige. This day should be devoted to her and no one else."

Hayden then walked away. As he made his way outside, his friend Dan caught up with him.

"What the fuck was that all about, man?" Dan asked.

"Nothing... let's just go," Hayden responded as he walked toward the parking lot.

They got into Hayden's car and pulled out of the lot. Neither of them noticed that Kali had come outside and was watching them pull away. Dan drove Hayden and himself the short five-minute ride to the cemetery. As Hayden stepped out of the car, he looked across the sprawling fields of grass, interrupted every few feet with headstones. He thought about how each granite or marble slab was a physical representation of a moment of grief for a different family. As everyone assembled on the knoll overlooking the piece of earth that they would soon bury Paige in, Hayden stood silent with Dan, Abby, Clark, and Samantha by his side. He made a point to avoid speaking to Kali again.

As the pastor said a few more words, Hayden scanned the attendees and could see the way that Paige had impacted each of their lives. Paige's mother and father spoke briefly, at times almost unable to continue through the sobs and tears. Paige's father motioned to Hayden to come up to the lectern. They had requested that he say a few words before Paige was buried. Hayden walked up and took his place, looking out at the mourning group again and briefly making eye contact with Kali. As Hayden began to speak, he attempted to keep his voice steadfast and unwavering despite the rippling of emotion tearing through him.

"Paige has been my dear friend since we were eleven years old. She never faltered in her oath or her bond as one of the few people that would unequivocally support and love me. I sincerely hope that she would say the same about me. In truth, we were much closer to being family than friends. She rooted for my success as she passionately pursued her own. Every person standing here today has had their lives positively changed just by her presence. In an attempt to placate our grief, many people often turn to phrases like 'everything happens for a reason' or 'she's in a better place now.'"

Hayden paused to clear his throat and look out over the crowd. Dan clutched his hand close to his chest and gave Hayden a thumbs-up gesture.

"However, as I stand here today, ready to bury my friend that gave so much of herself to others and asked so little in return, I find myself questioning the powers of this world who have deemed it fair that they take Paige from us. One thing that I know in my heart is that Paige would want everyone here today to take something away from this moment, something that they could use as a catalyst to push their own lives forward… since her ability to do that was cut short."

Again pausing, Hayden took a sip of water before continuing to soothe his increasingly raspy voice and get a handle on his rising emotions.

"We sit around daily and think about all of the things we need to change, our shortcomings… and how we can make ourselves better people, how to improve our lives. But that's the thing, we're complacent. We dream of ourselves as this image of continually improving, ever-evolving in our struggle, yet we don't. We remain comfortable in our day-to-day lives, never changing a thing... Until one day, thirty, forty, fifty years from now, when we're lying in a hospital bed, in our last minutes, with the few people we've managed to keep by our side, lamenting to ourselves and to them that if we only had the chance, we would do it all differently. Paige didn't wait, she took that chance every day, and she continually achieved great things. For all of us here, we do have the chance. Today is the chance, and it may be the last one you get. Take it or leave it."

As Hayden walked back to his spot next to his friends, the silence of the crowd indicated a mixture of contemplation and a slight shock at his words. Hayden drew in a deep breath and released it in a sigh, no longer attempting to hold back the tears that had been welling up in his eyes during his entire speech. Abby put her arm around Hayden in an attempt to comfort him.

"A little unconventional, but I liked it," Dan whispered to him and patted Hayden on the shoulder.

The burial proceeded, and soon Hayden found himself standing in an almost empty cemetery. Abby and Dan stood next to him while Hayden silently reflected on the life of his friend. After thirty minutes of somber silence, Hayden placed a rose on Paige's headstone, and the three friends made their way back to the parking lot.

જી જી જી જી જી જી

Kali arrived that evening at her hotel room, pondering what

Hayden had said and considering her choices in the past. She had felt guilty about just up and leaving everyone behind, especially Hayden. It was really the worst of circumstances for her to be reconsidering this, yet here she was, wondering why she acted the way she did a couple years ago.

As she lay in bed, she noticed herself drifting into a stream of thoughts. She missed the nights that she and Hayden spent in his bed. His plain white sheets, the press of his lips against her cheek, and the scraping of his unshaven face against her soft skin. Her thoughts ran away from her, recounting all the times she and Hayden spent together. She realized how profoundly she missed him over the years… and that she might have just let him slip away. She acted like she was fine at the funeral. Yet, now that she was alone, aided by nothing more than the dim light from the hallway peeking from under the door, she knew that she couldn't postpone any longer what she had tried to relegate to the existential backburner… she needed to make up with Hayden.

Her thoughts flickered to memories of the two of them… sneaking into concerts at the Irvine Meadows, Hayden flying her out to New York for a few days while he was there for a conference just because he thought that she would love the city as much as he did, and of course the frequent patronizing of local dive bars where they didn't care to check your ID as long as you kept your cool. The thoughts brought her mixed feelings of happiness and regret.

As she exhaled heavily, representing her indecisiveness in her forthcoming actions, Kali leapt up out of bed and walked over to the bathroom. The hotel's water heater exhibited its efficiency as Kali turned on the shower, steam instantaneously billowing over the top of the glass enclosure. As she returned to the bedroom and undressed, Kali placed a phone call to the reception desk. Wandering back into the bathroom, she shot off a succinct text message before stepping into the near-scalding water.

ര‍ ര‍ ര‍ ര‍ ര‍ ര‍

Unbeknownst to Kali, Hayden was nearby in the city. He had asked Dan to drop him off so that he could walk around and think. His friend obliged, acknowledging what he must be going through at the time. As Hayden walked through downtown, he thought about Kali, the service for her sister, and what the future held.

"If only I had gone to Yosemite with Paige and her family, I might have been able to keep her safe. She could still be here with us today," Hayden thought, letting his inner monologue run unabated even though he knew that it was pointless to concentrate on what-ifs. "Now I have the added stress of everything unraveling with Kali again when we have finals coming up next week."

Hayden felt a chill run through him as he continued on, even though it was quite warm outside. It was like he could feel the presence of Kali nearby. In fact, she was gazing out her window at the night sky and the city's skyline at the moment he was unknowingly walking by her hotel building.

The chill intensified for Hayden, a feeling he knew all too well by now. This time it was met with light… As the chill hit him, power flowed through him, and an intense white light emanated from his body straight up into the evening sky. It lasted only several seconds, but from fifteen stories above, Kali noticed the strange light flooding the street and skyline as she spoke to the front desk agent on her room's phone. She didn't know where it came from but figured it was just a spotlight from a nearby concert or club.

Meanwhile, Hayden looked around the street to see if anyone noticed the display of light or suspected him of whatever had just happened. There weren't many people around, and everyone on the street proceeded as if nothing unusual had happened.

"I really need to focus on mastering when these powers activate," he thought.

———

Hayden's thoughts were interrupted by the chime of his cell phone. He reached into his pocket and grabbed it. It was a text from Kali.

"Come over?" the text read.

Hayden took a moment to let the words of the text message sink in. Just a few hours ago, he and Kali had ended their interaction in what he would call the worst possible way. Was she seeking to continue the fight, he wondered. Hayden warily decided to make the journey to her hotel and fired off a response to her text to ask where to meet her.

The lobby of Kali's hotel was brimming with activity as Hayden made his way over to the front desk.

"I believe there should be a key card waiting for me?" Hayden asked the front desk agent in an inquisitive tone. "Kali Henderson would have left it for me."

"Yes, Mr. de Vere, I see that request right here," the agent replied as she grabbed a card from the desk drawer and programmed it. "Room number 15126 and the elevators are right over there at the rear of the lobby."

Hayden thanked the front desk agent for her help and made his way over to the elevators, just in time to get into an elevator car beside a small family before the doors closed. Hayden pressed the button for the fifteenth floor. The family's daughter, who looked to be about seven years old, excitedly pressed the button for their floor and exclaimed. "Mommy, we're on the floor right above him!" Hayden shot the girl a smile and chuckled. The girl's mother laughed and asked Hayden to excuse her daughter's outgoing behavior. "It's no problem at all," Hayden replied with a laugh.

The elevator chimed with its arrival on the fifteenth floor, and Hayden departed from the car, wishing the family a good night and giving a friendly wave to the little girl. He took a moment to observe the sign on the adjacent wall that pointed out the direction of the room numbers. As he made his way down the long hallway toward Kali's door, he began to feel a tinge of nervousness, just as he did at the church earlier that day.

Hayden removed the key card from his pocket and slid it into the door of room 15126. The electronic lock beeped, and a green light flashed, indicating that the door was unlocked and ready for him to enter. Hayden pushed the door open and made his way into the room, the slight nervousness now growing to the feeling of a pit in his stomach.

"Why am I so nervous all of a sudden?" Hayden asked himself.

The sound of the shower turning off as Hayden entered the room explained why he hadn't yet seen anyone present. Hayden walked across the room and stood next to the floor-to-ceiling windows.

"Kali, I'm here!" Hayden said in a raised voice so he could be sure that she would hear him from the bathroom.

"Okay, be out in a minute," Kali replied.

Hayden kept his position near the window and stared out into the night sky for about ninety seconds before he heard the sound of the bathroom door opening. Hayden turned around to see Kali standing in the doorway… she was nude, her damp hair just freshly brushed out, with droplets of water running off her body in places that she hadn't quite dried off completely. Hayden's eyes widened at the sight, and he found himself at a complete loss for words.

Kali grinned mischievously at Hayden and sauntered over to the bed in the middle of the room. As she sat down on the edge of the bed, Kali motioned with her hand for Hayden to come over to her. He promptly obeyed Kali's summons and walked over to where she was sitting.

As Hayden neared, Kali reached out her hand and grabbed his. Falling back onto the mattress, her grip pulled Hayden over her in a sensually fluid motion, culminating as she pulled him in for a kiss.

Hayden, still in shock from the unfolding entanglement, obliged to let his actions be completely guided by Kali's whims. Once their lips touched, Hayden's instincts returned, and he joined her in the effort of the kiss. This was not at all what he had envisioned occurring that night, but he went along with every moment as Kali removed his clothes and drew him back over her. Hayden took a moment to pause and look into her eyes just before they indulged in each other.

Several minutes later, any remnants of shower water on Kali's body had been replaced with sweat. Hayden lay on the king-size bed beside her, still partially in shock from the completely unexpected turn of events that night. The duvet lay crumpled at the foot of the bed, and the pillows were strewn about like an epic windstorm had made its way through the room. Kali had one hand running through her still-damp hair and the other hand futilely attempting to steady her shaking thighs.

"Wow," Kali finally broke the silence of the moment.

"That's an understatement..." Hayden replied. "That was absolutely amazing, Kali. The complete surprise of it definitely added to the effect also."

"I've been thinking about us all day since you left the church. I guess I finally came to my senses," Kali responded as she moved closer to Hayden.

Kali nestled her head in between Hayden's shoulder and neck, beginning to cuddle, her bare chest pressed against his side and one of her legs draped over his. Hayden noted the flashback of this feeling in his mind… recalling the faintly-familiar feeling of post-coital heat emanating from Kali's chest and groin on his skin. He reached over and flicked off the one remaining lamp in the room, and the two of them drifted off to sleep together, entangled and nude, for the first time in just over two years.

AGENTS OF FATE

أرض

Chapter Six

Finals Week

Kali and Hayden woke at 4:00 a.m. to the sound of a chorus of car alarms. They quickly noticed the jolting feeling of an earthquake shaking the hotel. After sitting in the bed until the rumbling stopped, they gathered their clothes and put them on as they walked over to the window. Pulling open the curtains, the early morning landscape of the city was largely devoid of activity. A handful of nearby parked cars still lit up the parking lot with flashing lights from their alarms. A few of the taller trees were still slightly swaying in testament to the seismic activity.

"Wow, that was a pretty strong one," Kali remarked to Hayden.

Yeah, not too bad," Hayden replied as he grabbed the remote and turned on the television.

Tuning into a local news channel, Kali and Hayden sat in the bed and listened as the anchor and several reporters explained that several earthquakes had struck the state in the last hour. Apparently, fault lines up and down California had all become active. The reporter on the screen alluded to the possibility that the "ring of fire" may be acting up.

After learning that the earthquake in their area was a magnitude 6.2, Hayden and Kali decided to go back to sleep for a few more hours.

At 9:00 a.m., Kali awoke first and made her and Hayden a couple cups of coffee with the in-room machine. The aroma filling the room pulled Hayden from his slumber, and he joined her on the sofa. As they sipped on their coffee, Hayden admitted that he had not expected Kali to ask him over.

"I'm obviously glad you asked me to come here," Hayden started. "I'm just wondering what this means as far as… us?"

"Well, my semester just ended," Kali explained. "So last night, I was thinking that maybe I'll just stay down here for a while, and you and I can figure out where we want to go from here. I'm open to exploring some possibilities if you are."

Hayden's demeanor perked up at the implication that Kali was spelling out. After two years of feeling nothing but confusion turned into despondence, he was suddenly hopeful. With this revelation, Hayden felt as if new blood was flowing through his veins. A chance to right the wrongs of the past and finally explore the potential that he and Kali had.

"That would be amazing," Hayden told her. "Not to be presumptuous, but if you need a place to stay, you're obviously welcome at my apartment."

"Trying to move me in after one night, Hayden?" Kali joked with him as she drank the last bit of coffee in her cup.

"Well, it was one hell of a night, to be honest," Hayden continued in the humorous dialogue. "For real, though, but only if you want to."

"Actually, yeah, I'm down to stay with you," Kali responded after a moment of thought. "If you get tired of me, then I can always find my own place."

Hayden rolled his eyes as he sipped the final drops of his coffee and stood up. As he walked across the room, he muttered, "Like there's a chance of me getting tired of you."

Kali remained sitting on the sofa and smiled, with her feet pulled up onto the cushions and her knees tucked up by her chin. She watched as Hayden strolled across the hotel room and over to the bathroom. Kali heard the sound of the shower coming on just before Hayden reappeared in the doorway.

"Shower?" he asked her half inquisitively and half seductively.

Kali answered his question by removing her shirt and throwing it across the room at him.

"I'll take that as a no," Hayden joked.

Kali got up from the sofa and ran towards him, laughing. When she arrived to meet Hayden in the doorway, she kissed him for a few moments, then pulled away to tease him.

She pulled her shorts down over her hips and let them fall to the tile floor, then walked past Hayden to the shower. "Are you still taking this as a no?" she joked back at him sarcastically.

"Definitely not," Hayden said as he watched Kali step into the shower. He quickly removed his clothes and joined her.

As Kali began her post-shower rituals to get ready for the day, she asked Hayden what he had planned.

"Well, I'm going to have Dan come pick me up because he has my car," Hayden informed her as he worked on packing items in her suitcase for her. "Did you want to ride with us back to the apartment? Or we can drop you off somewhere if you need to do something."

"Actually, Abby and Samantha asked me yesterday if I would go have a girls' lunch with them today after I checked out of the hotel," Kali replied.

"Oh, okay, that's cool. If you need me to pick you up later or anything, just let me know."

As Hayden filled Kali's suitcase with some of her surplus clothing, his phone chimed with a text message from Dan. Hayden swiped the notification open to see that Dan had just pulled into the hotel's parking lot.

"Dan's here," he informed Kali before following with, "You okay?"

"Yeah, I'm okay, you know, considering…" she assured him. "I'll give you a call after lunch. Thank you for packing my stuff up for me."

Hayden kissed her and then proceeded out of the hotel room to the elevators. After a short wait, the elevator car arrived. He stepped inside and pressed the button for the ground floor. As he stepped back, he felt a sudden sharp pain in his side that almost brought him to his knees. Hayden lifted his shirt to find that the piece of rock embedded under his skin was glowing with a distinctly orange hue. The pain subsided almost as quickly as it had come on, along with the luminescence.

"Well, that's concerning," Hayden said aloud to himself.

The elevator rang as it reached its destination in the

hotel lobby. Hayden drew in a deep breath and decided to ignore the strange phenomena for now. He walked out to the parking lot and met Dan, who was blaring "Out of Time" by The Weeknd as he sat with the window rolled down under a large tree.

As Hayden climbed into the passenger seat, Dan turned the stereo down and looked over at him as if to study his friend.

Dan broke the silence as he began to drive out of the parking lot. "Soooo… did you guys…"

Dan didn't have to finish the question, as Hayden could easily detect the implication from the look on his face.

"A lady never tells," Hayden joked in response.

"So that means yes," Dan said as he laughed.

"Maybe we just talked all night," Hayden feigned disgust at Dan's assumption.

"Dude, you guys have like two years of built-up sexual tension," Dan was unwavering in his analysis of the situation. "I'll be surprised if Kali doesn't get a bill from the hotel for a broken bed."

"Subtle," Hayden said as he shook his head at Dan.

"One of my many fine qualities," Dan joked.

"She's going to stay with me at my place," Hayden revealed to him. "At least for a while. We're going to see what happens."

"Wow, that's actually really good news! You must be happy."

"It is," Hayden replied. "I think we might actually have a chance at being together."

"That's cool, bro," Dan said. "I hope it works out. I don't want to see you in the same state you were in two years ago when she left."

"You know if it doesn't work out now, it'll be different," Hayden mused. "At least they'll be a coherent reason behind it this time."

"True," Dan agreed.

The two carried on their conversation as they grabbed a quick lunch at a local sandwich shop, then headed back to Dan's apartment. Hayden stuck around for a few hours watching a movie with Dan and discussing plans for the summer before Kali called to let him know her girls' day was wrapping up.

The television quietly filled the background with reports of aftershocks and several other earthquakes in other parts of the world. Hayden and Dan ignored it as they made a plan for lunch after the following day's Chemistry final. Hayden then took off and headed to pick up Kali in downtown Fullerton.

As they arrived back at Hayden's apartment, he received a text from Armond about the recent earthquakes.

"Dan already?" Kali inquired as they walked in the apartment's front door.

"No, it was Armond," Hayden replied, forgetting that she didn't know who that was until he saw the confused look on her face. "Oh yeah, you don't know him yet. You'll meet him tomorrow. A new friend of ours."

"So do you think that maybe we'll have time to do a little shopping tomorrow?" Kali asked, pointing to her singular suitcase. "I didn't exactly bring a lot with me, and all the rest of my stuff is in storage up in Tacoma."

"Yeah, of course," he said. "I have my Chem final at 10:00 a.m. Then Dan wants us all to go to lunch together afterward. We aren't meeting up with Armond until 4:00, so we can go shopping before that."

As they relaxed on the couch, Kali told Hayden about her day with Abby and Samantha. For the next few hours, they continued in various conversations about their lives for the previous two years until Hayden noticed he was again getting hungry. As Hayden cooked dinner, Kali unpacked her suitcase.

"You can move my stuff around in the closet and the dresser to make room for your things," he told her. "There's still plenty of room in both."

Kali smiled at him as she carried her clothes down the hallway. She placed her few outfits on hangers in the closet, put a small assortment of bras, socks, panties, and shorts in the dresser drawers, and then tossed her dirty laundry in the hamper. Kali noted the absence of signs that other females had recently been in the apartment.

As she made her way back to the kitchen area, she asked Hayden. "So, no girlfriends or anything?"

Hayden laughed. "Nope, honestly, I haven't even been on a date in like six months."

"Oh, so just casual…" Kali insinuated mischievously.

"All I do is go to class and then hang out with the group," Hayden replied while giving her a look. "You know, I barely get time to breathe with my major."

"Still planning on going to med school after you graduate, then?" she asked.

"Yep, that's still the plan," Hayden confirmed as he finished preparing dinner. They sat down and slowly ate while sipping their way through a bottle of wine and talking more about life after college.

After eating and cleaning up the dishes, they returned to the bedroom to relax. As Hayden lay down on the bed and turned on the television to find a movie or documentary, Kali went to the bathroom to take off her makeup and prepare for sleep.

Hayden continued to flip through the possible entertainment selections on the television until Kali walked out of the bathroom, and his attention was immediately drawn to her standing nude in the doorway. She let him stare for a few moments before she walked towards the bed.

"I've been trying to control myself all day, you know," she said as she walked closer.

Hayden's eyes grew wider as he understood her intentions, followed by a grin that communicated his level of excitement. He abandoned even the faintest of interest in the television as Kali crawled over him on the bed and kissed him. If there was any doubt as to what she wanted, she quickly dispersed it as she initiated intercourse.

Afterward, Hayden turned off the lights, and he and Kali cuddled as they fell asleep, now satisfied and exhausted.

Several hours later, Hayden bolted awake to another searing pain in his side. He clutched his abdomen and looked over at Kali, who was still sound asleep. Hayden got out of bed and walked to the living room, where he fell to his knees in pain. As he examined the source of the pain, the shard of rock again began to glow orange, now radiating brighter and then dimmer. He grabbed his phone from the floor beside him and dialed Armond.

"Hayden?" Armond groggily answered. "What's going on?"

"That sharp piece of rock that Paige stabbed me with…" Hayden replied through the pain. "It's randomly hurting, and it's like glowing orange. This is the second time today that this has happened."

Armond was silent for a few seconds before he spoke. "This must have something to do with all of the earthquakes, with the Alva'ci."

"What do you think is happening? Can we take this thing out?" Hayden inquired.

"I'll take a look at it," Armond replied. "Do you think you'll be okay until we all meet tomorrow?"

"Yeah, I think so," Hayden said. "The pain is starting to go away now. It only lasts for a few minutes at a time."

"Alright, try to get some rest until then," Armond continued. "Let me know if it happens again."

They ended the call, and Hayden made his way back to bed. He was glad that Kali remained asleep, and he crawled back into bed next to her.

Hayden awoke to his alarm at 9:00 a.m. and was met with the smells of coffee and pancakes drifting down the hallway from the kitchen. He pulled on a pair of pajama shorts and walked down the hallway. Hayden stopped near the dining room table to observe Kali, who had not yet seen him. She was dancing in place to the music playing in her headphones as she flipped pancakes, dressed in just a crop top shirt and a pair of panties. Hayden was smiling as he walked over to her. She pulled her headphones out and returned the smile.

"Wow, I might have to keep you around," Hayden said jokingly as he gave her a kiss on the lips.

"If you're lucky," she quipped back at him. "Or at least if you keep doing what you did last night," she followed up with a mischievous smile.

Hayden playfully smacked her butt as she walked by to pour him a cup of coffee. "Well, I can hold up my end of that bargain," he returned the flirtatious innuendo.

"You keep it up, and maybe I'll start cooking breakfast in the nude," she said, looking back over her shoulder at him with the same grin still painted on her face.

"You do that, and you might become the breakfast," Hayden kept it going.

Kali walked over to him and placed her finger over his lips. "Shut up, Hayden," she told him in a serious tone. "If you keep talking, we're going to end up on top of the dining room table... and you have a final to go to in less than an hour."

As if to reinforce the gravity of her words, she ended her speech by grabbing his hand and placing it over the gusset of her panties. Her level of arousal was made instantly evident to Hayden.

"Yeah…" Kali simply said as she loaded pancakes onto their plates. "Unfortunately, we don't have time for that."

"Well, while you're putting syrup on those pancakes, I'm going to go ahead and grab the 'wet floor' sign, so no one slips and falls," Hayden went back to joking with her.

Kali responded by throwing a wad of paper towels at his head.

"I think you need those more than I do," he continued.

Now Kali glared at him with feigned malice. Hayden walked over to her, grinning. He grabbed a bite of pancake from the nearest plate and placed it in her mouth. As she obediently began to chew it, he spun her around to face the counter.

"I live two minutes away from the college," he whispered in her ear as he pulled her panties down.

Kali gasped as Hayden proceeded to fulfill her wishes.

ɛɔ ɛɔ ɛɔ ɛɔ ɛɔ ɛɔ

After quickly eating the slightly cold pancakes, Hayden took a lightning-fast shower and rushed to the college to take his Chemistry final. He entered the classroom right on time and took a seat next to Dan. For the first ten minutes of the test, Hayden didn't write anything. Instead, he found himself lost in thought, replaying scenes from the morning in his head.

Dan finally tapped Hayden on the arm to pull him out of his daze. Hayden nodded at him as a thankful gesture and got to the test. Fifty minutes later, the test time was up, and Hayden walked to the front of the classroom and placed his test on the professor's desk. After a quick comment from the professor on how well Hayden had done in the class that semester, he was out the door and joined Dan in the hallway.

As they walked to the elevator, Dan joked to begin the conversation. "Piece of cake test, right?"

"It wasn't too bad," Hayden replied.

"A little bit harder when you spend the first ten minutes spacing out, though," Dan jabbed at Hayden. "What was that all about?"

Hayden chuckled and told him, "Oh, just going over the morning in my head, I guess, and lost track of what I was supposed to be doing."

"The morning?" Dan inquired, his attention now piqued. "What was so special about this morning?"

Hayden gave Dan a look before continuing the

conversation. "Kali got up early and made me breakfast..." he hesitated for a moment. "...and we had a little fun, I suppose."

"I knew it!" Dan exclaimed a little too loudly for the hallway.

Hayden rolled his eyes and mockingly told him, "Okay, detective, congratulations."

"So you guys are like officially back together then, or what?" Dan asked.

"I mean, I suppose so," Hayden thought before saying it aloud. "We discussed giving things a try again, so yeah."

"That's cool, bro. I'm happy for you guys," Dan conceded. "Is Kali meeting us for lunch then?"

"Yeah, she said that she was going to walk over to campus about ten minutes ago and meet us at the food court," Hayden informed him as they exited the building and started to make their own way over to their lunch spot.

As the duo approached the food court, they spotted Kali sitting with Abby, Samantha, and Clark at a table near the middle of the busy area. They walked up and sat down to discuss what to eat.

"Hey, guys!" Kali exclaimed, then continued after giving Hayden a kiss. "How did the chemistry final go?"

"It was no big deal," Dan replied. "Me and your boy

Hayden here are chemistry masters."

Hayden laughed at Dan's confident answer, not because he was incorrect but because they both did seem to possess a relative knack for the subject.

"Good to hear," Abby chimed in. "Just a few more finals to go, right?"

Hayden nodded in agreement as he scanned the familiar options in the food court, trying to decide what he was craving. "Yeah, I've got four more tests this week. Tomorrow is microbiology, Wednesday is physiology, and Thursday is modern physics and psych."

"I don't know how you stay sane with all those classes," Clark interjected. "That much science would kill me."

"Hayden's just a robot, bro," Dan jokingly answered in place of Hayden. "I swear his brain is hooked up to Google or something."

"If I was a robot, I wouldn't be so damn hungry right now," Hayden joked back. "Let's get some food."

Everyone nodded their heads in agreement and stood up to get in line for their chosen meals. After an hour of eating and conversing, the group split up and went their separate ways after Hayden reminded Dan and Abby to meet him and Kali at Armond's place in the evening.

಴ ಴ ಴ ಴ ಴ ಴

Hayden and Kali arrived at the local mall after making a quick stop at his apartment to drop off his backpack. Over the next three hours, Hayden accompanied her through several stores, watching her try on new clothes, pick out necessities, and purchase some personal care items. As they left the mall, Kali thanked Hayden for taking her.

They arrived back at Hayden's apartment and began filling Kali's section of the closet with her new outfits. By the time they finished, it was time for them to head to Armond's.

As they made the short drive, Kali inquired. "So, did this guy go to college with you?"

"Umm, no," Hayden replied. "He's more of an extra-curricular friend if you will."

"Mysterious," Kali joked.

"Yeah, you'll see once we get there," Hayden continued. "It's kind of a lot to explain."

Kali gave Hayden a look that seemed to mix both confusion and discontent in not being filled in. They arrived at Armond's and parked in the driveway, with Dan and Abby arriving immediately after them in his car. Armond walked out his front door to meet the group as they pulled up.

"Hello, everyone," Armond started. "Let's get right down to business, shall we?"

"Yeah, sounds good. Armond, this is Kali," Hayden said as they walked up to him. "...and Kali, this is Armond."

Armond shook Kali's hand and inquired. "You are Paige's sister, correct? I'm very sorry for your loss."

"Yes, and thank you," Kali replied as they walked into the house.

The group all took a seat in the living room around the coffee table. Armond brought several cups from the kitchen along with a pitcher of iced tea for everyone.

"So, it appears that there are four dead," Armond led into the conversation. "We were able to avert disaster, but I do not know if that means Hayden's additional powers will disappear and go to other holders to resume the spell holding the Alva'ci dormant."

"Okay, so what is all this about powers?" Kali interjected. "Are you guys actually serious?"

"You didn't tell her or show her?" Armond asked, looking at Hayden skeptically.

"We've been a little busy getting her new things for the apartment... and stuff," Hayden replied.

Armond quickly filled Kali in on the basics of the Alva'ci, the powers, and what had happened with her sister Paige. She still had a look of disbelief on her face after hearing the onslaught of hardly believable information.

"Let's go to the backyard, and Hayden can show you," Armond said as he motioned to Kali and Hayden.

The entire group got up and gathered in the backyard to see the oncoming spectacle. Armond set up some spare pieces of wood about twenty-five feet in front of the group and looked over at Hayden to indicate that he could begin at any time.

Hayden raised his right hand, and the symbol of Electricity started to glow. He pointed at one of the boards that Armond had set up with his pointer and middle fingers. Instantly, a bolt of lightning flowed from his fingertips and hit the board, splitting it into pieces.

Kali was already awestruck with the first display of his powers, but Hayden continued on. The symbol of Fire now replaced the symbol of Electricity on the back of his hand. A momentary stream of fire engulfed a second piece of wood until it was nothing but ash. Hayden then raised his hand up toward the sky, and a blinding white light shot straight up from his palm.

Armond picked up a nearby rock to help demonstrate the final acquired power. While Hayden was still facing away from the group, Armond threw it in his direction. Sensing the sudden kinetic energy heading toward him, Hayden turned and raised his hand. The rock stopped mid-air before reaching Hayden and then fell to the ground.

"Yeah, so that's it," Hayden said to the group as he walked back over to join them.

"Let's go back inside and discuss our final topic," Armond told everyone as he motioned to the door.

The group made their way inside and once again took their places around the coffee table. Hayden remained standing because he was aware of what was coming next.

"Hayden, if you will," Armond instructed him.

As he walked into the center of the group, Hayden removed his shirt. The shard of rock implanted in his side was visible to all, and they stared at it as Armond approached Hayden.

"So you've been having random pains emanating from this shard?" Armond asked him.

Kali interrupted and directed her complaint to Hayden. "Wait, you never told me about any pain!"

"Yes, it has happened a couple of times now, and the shard glows orange when the pain comes," Hayden answered them both at once and then continued to address Kali. "I didn't tell you right away because I didn't want you to be all worried about me. It lasts for a few minutes and then goes away."

Kali let out an exasperated sigh to vocalize her

disappointment and disagreement with Hayden's analysis of the situation. Armond approached Hayden to have a closer look at the shard.

"All that I do know for certain is that this shard of rock is from the cave where Paige passed away," Armond mused aloud as he peered at Hayden's side. "It must have some kind of connection to the Alva'ci, but I am not entirely sure what that connection is. I will have to read more about it."

Armond brought his hand closer to Hayden's skin at the location where the shard was implanted, and an orange glow started to pulsate from the shard. Hayden fell to his knees with the wave of oncoming pain and clutched at his side, which was now emitting an even stronger glow. Kali leapt from her seat and rushed over to him.

Armond and Kali helped Hayden to his feet and sat him in the nearest available chair. The room fell silent for the next two minutes until the shard stopped glowing, and Hayden indicated that the associated pain had dissipated. The air of uneasiness in the room was still evident in everyone's demeanor.

"What is concerning to me is that these pains appear to be coming on more often and at quicker intervals," Armond told Hayden as he ran his fingers through his beard in thought.

"Well, they should theoretically go away also when that spell is restored, right?" Hayden asked him.

"I would assume so," Armond agreed but didn't commit fully to the answer. "It is hard to say what will happen until we see it happening."

"Well, that's just about the least reassuring answer possible," Hayden said, half joking and half worried.

"Can't you just take it out of his side?" Kali asked Armond.

"We could attempt that, but I think it would be wise to wait until after the spell is restored and the Alva'ci is comatose once again," Armond replied to her. "If there is some kind of active connection between that rock and the creature, then attempting to remove it right now may put Hayden in danger."

"That's okay. We can wait," Hayden insisted. "This spell has gotta go back into effect sometime soon."

"Just keep me posted on your status," Armond told Hayden. "For now, let's call this meeting complete. Stay vigilant, and when this is all over, we can celebrate. My treat."

The group said their goodbyes and left Armond's house. Dan, Abby, and Hayden all needed to study for their following day's finals, so everyone went their separate ways for the night.

When Hayden and Kali arrived back at his apartment, she was still excitedly asking questions about his powers. Hayden tossed his car keys on the counter as they walked in and then sat on the couch in the front room. Kali remained standing, restless.

"So, is there anything else you can do," Kali asked him, then giggled as she continued her question. "Like, could you make my clothes disappear?"

"I'm afraid I would have to do that the old-fashioned way," Hayden jested. "I mean, I guess that I could burn them off."

Kali wasn't amused at that prospect. "Yeah, let's not try that," she said.

"So far, it's just the powers you saw at Armond's place," Hayden finally answered the first part of her question.

"Damn, how lucky am I," Kali said. "I already thought you were a pretty amazing guy, but now you're like some superhero or something."

"I don't know if I'd go that far," Hayden said, laughing.

"So, what are we going to do this summer?" Kali asked him, changing the subject. "Finals are almost over for all of you."

"Whatever you want to do," Hayden answered. "This weekend, I'm meeting my parents up in Camarillo at their friend's house for a little get-together, but after I get back on Sunday, we can do whatever your heart desires."

"Okay, I'm going to have a little girls' weekend with Abby while you're gone," Kali told him. "When you get back, maybe we can plan out a little vacation together or something."

"Now that sounds like a good summer," Hayden replied with a smile on his face.

"Hey, Hayden, you were my sister's closest friend," Kali abruptly changed the subject. "Do you think there was like any part of her left in there at the end?"

Hayden's posture visibly changed as the question hit him. "No. At the end, that wasn't her. That was some evil thing using her body. Your sister is at peace now," Hayden said as he placed his hand on Kali's shoulder in a reassuring gesture.

"You're right," she replied, placing her hand on his.

The remainder of the week seemed to fly by. Hayden and Dan, who shared many of the same classes, breezed through their remaining finals with relative ease. They accompanied Abby to a Wednesday evening dinner honoring her semester's achievements as the Computer Science

Department's STEM Scholar Award recipient.

Between all of the bustle of the last week of the school year, Hayden focused on refining his control over his powers and spending quality time with Kali. Friday night rolled around, and with it, a sense of accomplishment. After Hayden finished packing his bag for his Saturday morning trip to Camarillo, Kali grabbed him by the arm and led him to the bedroom to finish off the night with amorous intimacy before falling asleep.

AGENTS OF FATE

نار

Chapter Seven

When Among Ten

"When among ten, five shall fall…
the strength of their hand will be tested.
The trials of one led into darkness, shall prove the end of an era."

Saturday, June 18

Hayden pulled into the driveway of Gabe and Martha Hensley at their home in Camarillo. Hayden's father, Rick had met Gabe several years prior at an information technology convention in San Diego. Gabe had invited Hayden's father to bring the whole family over for a barbecue when they returned from the convention. At the gathering, Hayden's mother, Annie, immediately got along with Martha. Hayden recalled that ever since that day, the two families spent a fair amount of time together for holidays, cookouts, parties, and the occasional game night.

Hayden took a moment to recount the last time he had been to Gabe and Martha's home and surmised that it was for a gathering two weeks after he had departed his parent's house to attend college.

"Almost three years ago," Hayden thought to himself in amazement at how fast time had apparently flown.

Hayden and his younger brother Eddie had primarily hung out with Gabe and Martha's son Pete, who had just recently turned eighteen. On occasion, Hayden's younger sister Jillian and Pete's sister Elle would join the group on their random adventures gallivanting through the streets of Camarillo.

Hayden's father walked out to greet him as he exited his car and began to walk up the driveway to the Hensley's home. The two embraced in a hug before Rick offered his congratulations.

"Three years down, only one left to go!" Rick said.

Hayden laughed as he responded. "Yeah, one year left here and then on to another college for more."

"Hey, you'll breeze right through it, I'm sure," Rick replied. "Your mother told me that you said all the finals went really good."

"Oh yeah, nothing I couldn't handle," Hayden continued to joke with his father.

"Well, everyone is inside and ready, I think," Rick said as they began to walk up to the front door. "And we get two celebrations today instead of just one, so that's pretty cool."

Hayden's father was referring to both families' joint decision to celebrate Hayden's end of the semester along with Elle's birthday party since the two events happened to almost coincide.

"Honestly, the end of the school year isn't that major of a thing, Dad," Hayden told him. "You and Mom could have just taken me out to dinner or something, and Elle could've had the whole day focused on her."

Rick chuckled as the two walked through the front door. "Yeah, I know, Son. But Elle doesn't mind, and her party isn't until the afternoon."

As Hayden entered the front room, he scanned the area full of familiar faces. His mother rose from her seat on the couch and immediately walked over to give him a hug. Martha soon followed and welcomed Hayden, telling him congratulations on another year finished in his undergraduate work.

Gabe and Pete waved at Hayden from the kitchen, where they were working on an elaborate breakfast for the group. Hayden returned the wave and thanked them for their generosity. Elle was sitting in a recliner in the living room, her legs over one armrest and her head perched on the other as she scrolled through her TikTok feed. She glanced up when she noticed the commotion in the room and spotted Hayden.

Elle briefly shot Hayden a smile before getting up to properly welcome him.

"Happy birthday," Hayden offered as Elle approached him, handing her an ornately wrapped box.

"Thank you!" Elle delightedly replied as she shared a hug with Hayden. "You're almost done with college now, right?"

"One more year down there," Hayden told her. "But then I'll be on to my graduate program right after."

"Oh, do you know where you're going for that?" Elle inquired.

Martha approached. "Sorry for interrupting… but Elle, honey, can you go with Annie and me to get your cake?"

"Oh yeah, I'm ready to go," she replied to her mother, then turned her attention back to Hayden. "Tell me all about it later when my mom isn't dragging me all over town?"

"Of course," Hayden replied as he smiled and laughed.

Annie placed her hand on Hayden's shoulder as she walked out the front door with Martha and Elle. "We'll be back in about thirty minutes."

"Okay, I'll help everyone get breakfast finished up and ready. Love you, Mom," Hayden replied to her.

Gabe and Pete were chopping up ingredients for omelets when Rick and Hayden joined them in the kitchen.

"What can I do?" Hayden asked them.

"Why don't you start whipping up your French toast recipe?" Gabe responded. "You have some kind of magic touch with French toast… Pete and Elle both love it when you make it."

"That's true," Pete followed and then joked. "If you ever got bored in college, you could always just start a French toast food truck."

"That's not a bad idea," Hayden replied and went to work gathering the ingredients he needed. His father began making pancake batter.

Almost thirty minutes later, to the tee, Martha, Annie, and Elle returned through the front door with her birthday cake and some additional decorations they had found at the store. Elle immediately smelled the fragrances of cinnamon and vanilla wafting through the house over the other aromas and went running to the kitchen.

"Hayden, are you making me your French toast?" she gleefully exclaimed.

"You?" Pete quickly interjected. "You mean everyone."

Elle rolled her eyes at her brother. "I'm pretty sure it's all for me. It is my birthday party after all," she snarkily replied, while smiling at Hayden as if she were looking for him to agree.

"As much as you want," Hayden told her.

The breakfast preparations were complete within minutes, and everyone sat at the dining room table to enjoy a hearty meal to fuel the day's events. Hayden told the group about his finals before delving into the more serious topic of Paige's memorial service and how everyone in his group of friends was holding up.

ෆ ෆ ෆ ෆ ෆ ෆ

8:00 p.m. rolled around, and the last of the party guests left the Hensley's home. Pete bid farewell to everyone as he left with his group of friends to attend a concert for a local band. Annie and Rick joined Martha and Gabe in cleaning the aftermath of the day.

Hayden was sitting on a lounger in the expansive backyard near the pool. He watched as the sun began to make its way behind the hills, painting the sky with purple and orange hues throughout the light scattering of clouds along the horizon. His concentration was interrupted, and he looked over toward the house as he heard the doors to the back patio close. Elle walked toward him.

"Wow," she said in reference to the sunset. "No wonder you're out here."

"Yeah, it's a beautiful sunset, that's for sure," Hayden replied.

Elle sat down on the lounger next to Hayden. "So, now that everyone is gone, we can continue our conversation from this morning… if you want."

"Yeah, of course," Hayden chuckled as he replied. "Umm, so I'm going to UCI after I graduate down in Fullerton next year."

"Oh, so you'll still be close by," Elle said.

"Yeah, only a few minutes further away, not heading to the east coast or anything," Hayden responded.

"That's cool. How expensive is college going to be for you?" Elle asked.

"Honestly," Hayden replied. "Not that much… I have a full scholarship right now down in Fullerton that pays for my entire four years. When I go over to UCI, most of that will be paid for with scholarships and grants as well. Almost everything I've made working while I've been in school has gone into savings."

"Wow…" Elle paused for a moment. "You'll have to show me how to get those kinds of scholarships."

"Of course," Hayden said with a laugh. "Step one is definitely spending way too much time studying."

"Okay, sure," Elle replied sarcastically. "For you, step

one was just to be insanely smart with no effort… but enough about school! I'm going to go get us some ice cream, okay?"

"That sounds perfect," Hayden told her, then added. "Thank you, Elle."

Elle ran off into the house to grab two bowls overflowing with cookies and cream ice cream. Hayden leaned back in the lounger and, for a moment, contemplated how his friends were doing back in Fullerton. However, he quickly returned his thoughts to the present state of relaxation, enjoying some time away from all the madness that had taken root in his life as of late.

The gentle clinking of metal spoons against porcelain drew Hayden's attention back as Elle approached with their ice cream. She handed Hayden his bowl, and he noted that between the two of them, Elle must have dispensed an entire half gallon of ice cream. Chocolate syrup covered the numerous scoops. As they ate, they continued to talk. After about an hour, their parents made their way outside, and everyone joined in on several rounds of card games into the late evening.

❧ ❧ ❧ ❧ ❧ ❧

Hayden awoke in a cold sweat and an adrenaline-fueled panic.

The smell of smoke stung his nostrils as he gasped for air in the dark bedroom. He sat up in the bed and looked around the room as his eyes adjusted to the darkness. Everything appeared to be normal. The smell of smoke faded after a few moments as Hayden concentrated on recalling the dream that he had been having.

Brief images of fire and rubble flashed through his mind, but Hayden couldn't remember any context for the images from his dream. All he knew was that the nightmare was intense and had jolted him out of sleep. He got out of bed and grabbed his shirt from a nearby chair. He slipped the shirt on and walked down the hallway to the back door, stepping outside onto the patio to cool down in the mild night temperature and have a quick smoke.

As Hayden breathed in a drag of smoke from his cigarette, the sound of the back doors opening caught his attention. Elle, who had been asleep in the living room, had woken up when Hayden walked through. She stepped out onto the back patio in her pajamas and slippers, walking up to where Hayden was sitting.

"You okay?" she asked him.

"Sorry to wake you up," Hayden replied to her. "But yeah, I'm okay. Had a pretty intense nightmare, apparently. Just came out here to calm my nerves a little bit."

Elle sat down next to him. "What was it about?" she asked.

"The only thing I remember is just tiny bits of fire and like debris from something being destroyed," Hayden told her. "And as weird as it sounds, when I woke up, I swear that I smelled smoke."

"Sounds pretty horrible," Elle said, pausing for a moment before continuing. "I'll sit out here with you until you're done smoking if you want."

Hayden smiled at her, appreciating her concern and willingness to sit up with him in the backyard in the middle of the night.

"Thank you, Elle. I welcome the company," he replied and then proceeded to joke, "...you know, now that I think about it, maybe it was the gallon of ice cream you gave me earlier that gave me nightmares."

"Oh, shut up," Elle said as she pushed against Hayden's arm and playfully acted as if she had been insulted.

"I guess I really hadn't realized how long it's been since I've been around," Hayden admitted as he took a moment to ponder the past. "After I left for college and my parents moved out to their Nevada house full-time, I guess time just kind of flew by."

"You should take me up to Ventura in the morning,"

Elle suggested. "If you don't have to leave early, that is… and if you want to, of course. Remember how we all used to go and hang out by the beach?"

"I don't need to leave until the evening. So, yeah, I'd be happy to take you up there."

Elle's face brimmed with gleeful elation. "We can stop at the bookstore on the way, get some pizza, and then go over to the beach… okay?"

"That sounds like a nice way to wrap up the weekend," he agreed.

After Hayden finished his cigarette, the two walked back inside the house.

"Goodnight," Elle told Hayden. "I hope you sleep better now."

"Goodnight, Elle," Hayden replied. "Thanks for keeping me company. I'll see you in the morning."

Elle laid back down on the pull-out sofa and nestled herself under the blankets as Hayden made his way back to the guest bedroom. Hayden crawled into the bed and stared at the ceiling for a few minutes until he drifted off back to sleep. As he slept, a faint orange glow pulsed from his side through the bedsheets and blanket.

℘ ℘ ℘ ℘ ℘ ℘

Morning arrived, and Hayden was awakened by his father's knocking at the bedroom door.

"Breakfast!" Rick yelled through the door.

"Got it," Hayden replied groggily and readied himself to join everyone in the dining room.

After making a brief pitstop in the bathroom, Hayden arrived at the dining room table to see everyone already up and eating. This morning's breakfast was more toned down than the previous day's. The mood was leisurely at the table, with the exception of Elle, who was eating at a decidedly quicker rate than everyone else.

"In a hurry this morning?" Gabe asked.

"Yeah, kind of," Elle muttered in response with a mouthful of food. "Hayden is going to take me up to Ventura for a little bit today."

"Well, he just got out of bed. Give him a chance to eat first," Gabe joked. "If you choke on those pancakes, the hospital is the only place you'll be headed."

Elle huffed in mild disapproval at being chastised in front of everyone, even if only jokingly. However, noting that her father was correct in his observation, Elle slowed the pace of her eating so that Hayden didn't feel rushed.

"Isn't that better, now that you can actually taste the pancakes?" Gabe threw in one final jest.

______

Hayden filled his plate and sat down next to his mother at the table. The families continued through their meal while Rick, Annie, Gabe, and Martha planned a trip to the supermarket for a barbecue day by the pool.

An hour later, Hayden had finished getting ready and sat down in the front room to wait for Elle. He thumbed through the morning's newspaper until he heard Elle emerge from her bedroom. She walked down the hallway eager to depart, wearing her swimsuit under a pair of shorts and a t-shirt. As Hayden approached her, the floral bouquet scent with hints of vanilla floating through the air confirmed that Elle had indeed started wearing the eau de parfum that was part of his birthday gift to her.

"I love it," she effused, detecting Hayden's reaction to the aroma. "Are we ready?"

"We are ready."

Elle and Hayden arrived in Ventura twenty minutes later and made their first stop at a local bookstore on Main Street. Upon entering, Hayden was awash with memories of their fathers bringing them to the store at various times in the past. Elle fluttered about the store, gathering a handful of titles that struck her interest. Hayden primarily strolled through the aisles, watching Elle's chaotic approach to shopping. Reading had always been an interest that the two shared, so Hayden was never shocked to see Elle want to spend hours here. He eventually selected a book that Paige had told him about several months ago, but neither had found the time to purchase. As he read the back cover, Hayden looked up to see Elle standing next to him, all ready to go.

"Just one?" Elle was surprised that Hayden didn't have more books.

"I've been reading textbooks all year," he laughed. "Gonna ease my way into summer reading for now."

"I have a few books in my room that you might like too. You can take them back home with you."

"Oh, books from the library of Elle. I'm listening," Hayden jested.

"Well, as long as you don't wait another three years to come visit again," she added sarcastically.

"Okay, deal," Hayden relented, and they proceeded to the sales counter.

After Hayden purchased the books, the pair drove down Thompson Boulevard and made a quick stop for pizza before heading over to the beach for a few hours. Hayden enjoyed the relaxation that came from laying out in the sunlight and walking along the beach. After some mild effort, Elle convinced Hayden to wade out into the ocean with her. The two returned to the Hensley's home once Elle had sated her craving for a beach day. Back at the house, they joined their families out in the swimming pool.

❧ ❧ ❧ ❧ ❧ ❧

As evening approached, Hayden said his goodbyes to his mother and father, Gabe, Martha, Elle, and Pete. He spent the hour-and-a-half drive back to Fullerton reflecting on the weekend and was grateful that he was able to experience some relative peace amid all the recent tumult in his life.

As Hayden pulled his car into the driveway of his apartment, he noted the stillness in the air. As he stepped out of the car, Hayden looked up to see Kali coming outside to meet him. Hayden closed the door and was about to begin walking to meet Kali when a striking pain gripped his side, accompanied by the all-too-familiar orange glow from under his shirt. Kali began running towards Hayden as he fell to his knees, clutching at his side.

Hayden grimaced in pain and closed his eyes. The darkness was suddenly interrupted by the searing image of a figure surrounded by a fiery orange aura. The menacing vision sent a chilling fear racing through Hayden's mind. As he began to fall toward the ground, Kali caught him and sat him next to the car.

"Are you okay?" Kali asked him frantically.

Hayden opened his eyes, and the image of the figure disappeared. The pain subsided, but the glow under his shirt remained visible. He looked up at Kali, sweat now running down his forehead as if he had just run a mile in the summer sun.

"Yeah, I think so," Hayden said, trying to reassure her.

As Kali helped him to his feet, their balance was interrupted by a jolting tremor. The stillness in the air was replaced by swaying tree limbs and lampposts. In the distance, dogs barked in a chorus to the shaking earth.

After roughly a minute, the earthquake ended, and Kali led Hayden to the front door with her arm around him. As they made their way inside, Hayden sat down on the couch, and Kali filled a glass of water for him. As he sipped on the water, his cell phone rang. It was Armond.

"Already back to the madness," Hayden thought to himself.

As Hayden briefly spoke to Armond, he noticed that the orange glow from his side had subsided. Hayden ended the phone call and finished the glass of water.

"Armond told me that our earthquake wasn't the only one that just happened," Hayden told Kali. "Apparently, there were quakes up and down the entire west coast of the United States, Mexico, and Canada."

"Why do I get this horrible feeling that things are getting worse instead of better?" Kali remarked.

"It sure seems that way," Hayden agreed. "But Armond seems to think that everything should calm down and go back to normal in a matter of weeks."

"Well, I guess we'll just have to wait it out until then," Kali responded. "Do you want to lie down?"

"Sure," Hayden replied. "You can tell me about your weekend, and I'll let you know how mine was."

As they lay in bed, Kali recounted her weekend with Abby to Hayden, complete with details about their beach trip, shopping, and getting to know each other better over several meals and drinks. Hayden told Kali about his weekend in Camarillo.

"Sounds like you and Abby had a really good time," Hayden told her. "I'm glad you guys are becoming good friends."

"Yeah, it's nice," Kali replied, "...she's really cool. At first, I was afraid that it would be kind of awkward like I was kind of trying to replace my sister's presence as a friend, but we've actually really hit it off."

Hayden was speechless for a moment. Finally, he replied. "Yeah, I get that..."

Kali just sat and smiled at Hayden for a few moments

before continuing the conversation. "You know, I really missed you this weekend," she said, her tone now changing from conversational to slightly suggestive.

"Oh yeah?" Hayden jested in response.

"Yeah. A lot," Kali replied matter-of-factly, confirming her intent by placing her hand high on Hayden's thigh.

Hayden smiled at her, and Kali took that as her cue to take action. She removed her shirt as she moved from her place on the bed and sat on Hayden's lap. After the ensuing intercourse, highlighting their happiness to be back together after a weekend apart, the couple quickly fell asleep and forgot about the earthquakes and nightmarish images. A few hours into their slumber, Hayden's side began to faintly glow orange again as it had the night before.

Hayden woke in the morning to Kali lightly shaking him by the arm, concern marking her voice as she said his name. As he opened his eyes, he found Kali's attention alternating between his face and side. Hayden looked down to find that the shard embedded under his skin was steadily glowing, though this time, it was not accompanied by any of the tell-tale pain that seemed to be a hallmark of the occurrence.

"Hayden, look," Kali beckoned him as she noticed him waking.

He looked down to examine his side more closely. Not only was it glowing with the usual faint orange hue, but the color seemed to branch off from the shard. The phenomenon looked as though an orange-colored infection was seeping into his bloodstream and making its way through his circulatory system, with the shard as its epicenter. Hayden was once again slightly shocked to notice no feelings of pain. He got out of bed and examined himself more closely in the bathroom mirror. Although he was concerned, Hayden decided to wait and see if the glowing shard would become dormant on its own, just as it had every time previously.

As Hayden sat down in the dining room, Kali brought him a glass of orange juice and a bagel that she had been preparing in the kitchen. She then grabbed her meal from the counter and joined Hayden at the table.

"You should at least text Armond and see what he thinks about that," Kali insisted.

"Yeah, I suppose that you're right," Hayden replied. He put his bagel down on the plate and texted Armond a picture of the shard and the surrounding vein-like structures.

Hayden resumed eating the breakfast that Kali had made and waited for Armond to respond. As he gulped down the last of the orange juice, he was startled. The image of the orange aura-shrouded figure that he had seen over the weekend reappeared for a moment, this time with Hayden's eyes opened as if it were augmenting his normal vision. The image was gone in an instant, but the effect was enough for Kali to notice something was amiss.

"Are you sure that I don't need to take you to the doctor or something?" Kali asked him. "Maybe they can remove whatever that is."

"I think that's beyond their scope," Hayden replied. "I'm just going to rest some more. Thank you for breakfast. Can you let me know if Armond replies?"

"Yeah, of course," Kali told him, her voice still tinged with concern. "Do you want me to see if Dan or Abby wants to come over?"

"No, that's alright," Hayden replied. "I just need some rest."

Hayden proceeded back to the bedroom and lay down, feeling a distinct lack of energy even though he had just woken up. He drifted off to sleep and was met by a series of disturbing scenes vividly playing out in his dreams. The nightmarish movie that played out in his head was rife with destruction, panic, and death. Hayden saw his friends leaving him behind in the wake of a destroyed city as they sought their own safety. Suddenly, the dream changed to images of Hayden standing on a hillside that was riddled with bones while a fire blazed in the distance.

Immediately before being pulled from the nightmare, the vision changed to the image of the orange-auraed figure, rapidly increasing in intensity. As the images became crisper and clearer in his head, he felt that he recognized the figure as the Alva'ci. The creature spoke to him in a dark and menacing voice, telling Hayden to trust no one.

Hayden woke to the feeling that he was being torn from another plane of existence. He screamed out as he fell from the bed in a state of panic. Kali came running down the hallway and into the room to find Hayden on the floor, drenched in sweat and hot to the touch.

"Oh my God, Hayden," Kali exclaimed as she rushed to his side. "I'm going to have Armond and Dan come over."

"No," Hayden replied, attempting to downplay the seriousness of the situation. "It was just a nightmare… I'm fine."

Hayden struggled up to his feet and then sat down on the edge of the bed. In the back of his mind, the scene from his dream of his friends abandoning him led Hayden to subconsciously feel the need to be alone.

"Well, I didn't wake you up because I wanted you to get some rest," Kali told him. "But Armond replied a while ago. He seemed pretty concerned about the picture you sent him earlier. He wants to meet up as soon as possible."

"Fine," Hayden replied, his mind now slightly easing away from the dream-induced paranoia. "How long was I out for anyway?"

"Quite a while," Kali told him. "It's four o'clock in the afternoon now."

Hayden was surprised to hear that he had been asleep for that long. To him, it had felt like a matter of minutes. His mind continued to skip back and forth from reality to what he had seen in the dream.

"Babe, how about you go take a shower," Kali suggested. "Maybe it will help wash away some of the stress from today."

Hayden nodded his head in agreement with her and slowly walked to the bathroom. Kali watched as Hayden undressed and stepped into the shower, then made her way back to the front room. The veiled urgency that she felt was now readily apparent in her voice as she spoke to Armond on the phone.

Kali relayed to Armond what had happened when Hayden woke up, and he told her that he would be right over. She hung up and took a deep breath, attempting to calm her nerves. Kali decided to check on Hayden in the shower and let him know Armond was on his way to their apartment. As she entered the bathroom, Hayden was just stepping out of the shower to grab a nearby towel to dry off with.

"Armond is going to be on his way over," she informed him.

"Okay, babe," Hayden replied and began to dry off.

"I'm going to make you a sandwich real quick," Kali told him. "You must be hungry after not eating anything but a bagel all day."

Hayden smiled at her and nodded. "Thank you."

When Hayden appeared in the dining room, Kali had a freshly prepared turkey and ham sandwich waiting for him on the table, complete with pepper jack cheese, lettuce, to-matoes, and a slathering of mayo and mustard… just how Hayden liked it. He walked up to Kali and kissed her.

"Thank you, babe. I really appreciate everything that you're doing for me," he added before sitting down and be-ginning to devour the sandwich.

As Kali walked over and set a glass of soda on the table next to Hayden to accompany the sandwich, there was a knock on the front door. Kali opened the door and let Ar-mond and Dan into the apartment.

"Hey buddy, you alright?" Dan immediately queried.

"Yeah, I think so," Hayden told his friend. "Just a bad day is all."

Armond wasn't swayed by Hayden's dismissal of the

day's events and proceeded to walk up to Hayden, seeking to inspect the shard's status.

"Let's see," Armond said, almost in a demanding tone.

Hayden held a finger up to Armond and took the last bite of his sandwich before chugging down half the glass of soda. After he finished, Hayden stood and lifted his shirt.

"Nothing that crazy," Hayden insisted as Armond and Dan looked at the pulsating glow.

"What concerns me is that it almost looks as though the effects of the shard are somehow spreading," Armond disagreed, "...and Kali told me that you had some intense nightmares that left you in a rather rattled state."

"Yeah, some dreams about fires and destruction," Hayden informed him as he lowered his shirt. "But nothing that out of the ordinary for a nightmare."

Armond didn't relent in his growing suspicion that something was, in fact, out of the ordinary.

"I may have been wrong to assume that everything would go back to normal," Armond said to the group. "The influence of the Alva'ci should be waning. This activity with the shard and Hayden seems to suggest that the opposite is occurring."

"I did see an image flash in my head while I was dreaming," Hayden finally relented with the additional information.

"It was a figure surrounded by an orange glow. The feeling I had when I saw it was that the figure was the Alva'ci."

"So you're seeing it in your nightmares?" Armond mused.

Dan and Armond stayed at the apartment for a few more hours to observe Hayden and attempt to help ease Kali's nervousness. Everything appeared normal as the group gathered in the front room and began discussing possibilities for summer plans and which classes they would be taking in the upcoming semester.

As 8:00 p.m. rolled around, the group was beginning to feel much more at ease and looked at calling it a night. Hayden stood from his seat on the couch next to Kali to get a refill on their drinks. After a handful of steps toward the kitchen, Hayden froze in place.

"Babe, are you alright?" asked Kali.

Hayden's body shook as if an intense chill was running down the length of it. Kali, Armond, and Dan all stood and began to approach Hayden. As they neared him, the back of Hayden's hands were both lit with an intense orange glow. As Hayden raised his hands into the air, the kitchen window began to crack from top to bottom. Kali, Armond, and Dan looked at each other with confusion and worry evident on their faces.

"What's going on, Armond?" Dan asked, looking for an explanation of what was happening.

As the light on Hayden's hands dimmed, he fell to his knees. A sharp and sudden jolt in the ground threw everyone off balance as they approached Hayden to check on him. The ensuing earthquake pulsed with strong shockwave-like tremors for approximately a minute before it subsided. After it was over, Hayden came back to a state of normal consciousness, and Kali held him in her arms.

"Babe, what happened? Are you alright?" Kali pleaded as she tightened her grasp on him.

"I don't know," replied Hayden, confused. "I don't remember anything happening."

As Hayden rose to his feet and Kali helped him back to the couch, the faint noises of scared animals and errant car alarms echoed through the distant air. Without warning, Armond gasped and grunted as he clutched at his forehead, hinting at a sharp pain.

"Dude, not you, too," Dan remarked at Armond's sudden change of state.

"This is not good," Armond stated as he recovered. "That earthquake was widespread. A fifth agent of fate was killed in a landslide resulting from it."

"Wait, does that mean…" Dan began.

His sentence was interrupted as Hayden suddenly went limp and collapsed unconscious into the couch cushions.

"Hayden!" Kali screamed out in fear.

"Kali, keep an eye on Hayden," Armond requested. "I must leave for a while."

"Where are you going?" Kali protested. "He needs your help!"

"The remaining four agents of fate, the unknown ones…" Armond continued, his face now drained of color as a result of his fearful revelation. "They've become known to me with the death of the fifth. They are all making their way to my home. I have to meet with them. It seems that my worst possible fear is coming to fruition."

"I'll stay with you guys," Dan told Kali. "I'm here to help."

"If Hayden gets worse, call me immediately," Armond instructed them as he hurried out the front door.

AGENTS OF FATE

ماء

Chapter Eight

Darkness Consumes Me

Hayden was alone in pitch-black nothingness. As he waited for what seemed like an eternity for something to happen, he finally noticed a faint glimmer in the darkness. The dot of light appeared to be thousands of feet away from him, but after a few minutes, he noticed that it appeared to be slowly gaining intensity. He began to walk through the darkness toward the source of the light.

"What is this?" Hayden called out aimlessly into the darkness. No response.

Hayden continued to wander in the darkness until he remembered his powers. He wasn't sure if they would work or not, considering the fact that he was asleep, but he decided to make an attempt. The back of his hand glowed with the emblem of Light as he concentrated. Suddenly, the darkness was pierced by an enveloping column of white light.

Once Hayden's eyes adjusted to the scene, he was able to see that the darkness had now been replaced with a peculiar landscape. Behind him was a wasteland filled with dull grey grasses and haunting trees. In front of him was an elaborate room, its features all framed in black and orange. At the center of the room was a staircase, with a dark wrought iron cage located at the top of the flight. Inside the cage was the source of the light that he had seen in the distance, an orange-glowing orb of energy floating inside the bars. Hayden took a step forward but was immediately halted by a thunderous voice echoing across the room.

"The cognizant one," the voice boomed. "You may have won the battle against the shadow, but you cannot win the war that is coming."

"You're the Alva'ci?" Hayden directed his question at the orb floating inside the cage.

"This is but a minuscule piece of my essence," the orb responded. "Here to tell you that you have no hope of winning."

"Where is here exactly?" Hayden asked. "This is all just a dream. None of it is real."

"Ignorant human," the orb replied, then paused before continuing. "You don't even know your own powers. This is no idle dream. This is the dreamscape."

"You're right. I don't know what that is," Hayden said, seeking to draw out information from the orb.

"I know your powers better than you do yourself," the orb retorted. "This is why you cannot hope to overcome me. I will give you the opportunity to surrender here, now. I will allow you to save yourself and the one you love. Everyone else will die."

"How would you ever expect me to say yes to that proposition?" Hayden replied in defiant disbelief.

"It is a choice for you to either save yourself without fighting me," the orb said indignantly, "...or you can choose to fight me and die along with the rest of the planet. You are nowhere near powerful enough to defeat me, even with the other four holders of your ancient powers."

"You assume that," Hayden remarked.

"I know that," the orb barked back at him. "You had no knowledge of the dreamscape, which is a power of the Ane'illuminus that you've held all your life. You have had no clue that with this power alone, you've had the ability to rule over every person in your world."

Hayden was taken aback and left speechless for a moment. He processed the fact that this entity seemed to know much more than Armond did about the powers that he had.

"I can feel that you know I am right," the orb said, interrupting Hayden's thoughts. "I will show you how it all ends if you choose to fight me."

The room in front of Hayden faded away, and his body was forced by an unseen power into a stone chair that appeared behind him. Now the darkness that had taken the place of the room sprang to life with an oversaturation of colors and images. Hayden watched the unfolding scenes of carnage, destruction, and death as the orb showed him hundreds of variations of the future battle… all ending with Hayden watching as Kali, Dan, Armond, and his other friends and family members were killed. He shuttered each time he heard the screams from Kali just before she drew her last breath. Hayden watched his own death play out before each variation went black and immediately leapt into the next scene of gruesome possibilities. After what seemed like days to Hayden, the images in front of him finally ceased, and the darkness was soon replaced by the same room as before, with the cage and the orb.

"You see now the futility of your situation?" asked the orb.

Hayden was mentally exhausted and emotionally scarred from the relentless barrage of scenes that the orb had forced him to endure. He was bordering on the idea of defeat.

"I give up now, and you allow Kali and I to live?" Hayden asked.

Dan and Kali hovered about the front room, where Hayden was still lying unconscious on the couch. They mulled about for several hours in a mostly uncomfortable silence as they watched Hayden's eyelids move constantly, and his muscles twitch as if he was caught inside an interactive nightmare.

"Does this qualify as worse?" Dan asked, finally breaking the silence.

"Well, he is still normal as far as breathing, and he hasn't convulsed or anything," Kali replied.

"Yeah, alright," Dan conceded. "Let's give it some more time and see if he wakes up."

As they waited, Kali called Abby to give her an update on everything that had happened since they last saw each other.

"Is there anything I can do to help?" Abby asked over the phone. "I can come over and help you guys out."

"You don't have to right now," Kali told her. "It's really late, and there's really nothing happening at the moment. Dan and I would be happy to have you here if you want to come by in the morning."

"Of course. I'll try to be over there by like ten o'clock. I'm going to stop and check on Clark and Samantha first. I haven't heard from them since that last earthquake. I'll stop and grab some food and drinks on the way if you want me to."

"That would be wonderful," Kali replied with evident gratitude.

Dan handed Kali a refill of her coffee, and the two settled back into their seats to resume watching Hayden for any signs of change.

ଓ ଓ ଓ ଓ ଓ ଓ

Armond waited in the living room until the first knock on his door came at about midnight. He opened the door to find a young woman.

"Hi, I'm Lora," she said. "Something like clicked on in my mind and told me to come here."

"Good morning, Lora. My name is Armond," he replied. "Please come in and make yourself at home while we wait for the others to arrive."

Lora entered the front room and had a seat while Armond prepared a glass of water for her.

"Have you met any of the others yet?" Lora inquired,

trying to spark up a conversation.

"Only one so far," Armond told her, referring to Hayden. "He was the first to become known to me, and I traveled here from New York to meet with him."

"Oh, I'm from Denver," she added. "I guess there are probably some of us from all over."

Armond agreed with her assumption, and the two continued to get to know each other better for just over an hour before they heard another knock on the door. When Armond answered, he found two more agents had arrived at the same time. As they proceeded inside, Armond initiated introductions.

"Good morning, thank you for coming," he told them. "My name is Armond, and this is Lora. She is another wielder of the powers like yourselves."

The taller of the two new arrivals chimed in first. "Hi, my name is Mackenzie. I just flew in from Edmonton and I happened to run into Tiffany at the airport while I was waiting for a car."

The impromptu lead-in from Mackenzie prompted Tiffany to add her introduction to the group, "...that's me, Tiffany Woolf. I'm from Hinesville, Georgia. It's nice to meet y'all."

"So we're only missing one now," Armond continued

after everyone had taken a seat. "Hopefully they will show up soon, and we can delve into more of the specifics of what is happening. For now, I will bring some beverages and snacks if you like."

The group agreed to Armond's proposal, and he hurriedly went to the kitchen to gather an assortment of snack foods along with bottled water, soda, and iced tea.

A half-hour into snacks and conversation, the last attendee arrived at Armond's door. As he walked into the front room, he introduced himself.

"Good morning, I'm Shaun. Flew in from holiday in Cancun, originally from Mansfield in the UK," he stated.

Armond and the others took turns introducing themselves to Shaun, and they all settled into their seats. Armond began his crash course of why they were all there.

"All of you are aware that a power has awakened in you," Armond started, "...and all of you were drawn to come here tonight. I am going to explain to you why and I will also explain what these feelings of power are and how they will be needed in the immediate future."

"I feel some kind of power, but I have no idea what it is or what it means," Mackenzie chimed in.

"That is to be expected, Mackenzie," Armond replied. "Each of you has been bestowed with a latent ability. Before you, thousands of others have held these abilities. For tens of thousands of years, each person possessing these abilities, or powers, never knew they had them. This is because the powers only manifest in a specific threat's looming presence, which has never occurred before. So in the past, with the eventual death of a person who held one of these powers, it would then transfer to a new holder."

"So, we all kind of have superpowers or something?" Shaun asked, his interest now piqued.

"In a way, they could be considered that," Armond told the group. "About 56,000 years ago, many people possessed variations of these abilities, and they were able to use them in their everyday lives. Then one day, an alien lifeform arrived on the planet outside a small village in the middle east. It sought to erase human existence from the planet to allow the remaining members of its own species to claim it as their own. A group of the strongest and most agile magic users in the village attempted to defeat the threat, but even with all of their skills combined, they were only able to place the alien lifeform, called Alva'ci, in a comatose state deep underground."

After pausing for a moment to take a drink of water, Armond continued. "However, this victory came with a high price. In order to subdue the Alva'ci, a spell was cast that effectively eliminated the ability of humans to wield these magical powers any longer. The latent abilities that have been passed down through generations, and eventually to all of you, are only meant to be there as a remnant… a function of the continuance of the spell cast all those years ago. These remnants of power keep the Alva'ci in its comatose state."

"So what is the threat that is making all these powers manifest?" Tiffany vocalized what the entire group had been pondering.

"There are supposed to be ten of you. Ten holders of the remnants of the ancient powers, each person bestowed with one of the powers. Over the years, the texts handed down by my ancestors have often referred to the group of ten as the Agents of Fate. The reason for the powers being spread across ten separate people is to keep the effects of the spell sufficiently strong. Any time an agent of fate dies, there is a short window between that death and the next person receiving the powers. In order for the remnants of the powers to be effective in renewing the spell, they must be embodied in a human. So, spreading the powers across ten people allowed for the spell to remain in effect even if a few of the agents of fate died at the same time."

"So you said there's supposed to be ten of us," Lora interjected, "…and you said that there is one more of us that you know, who isn't here right now."

"Correct," Armond stated. "As of last night, only five agents of fate are alive. Four of the others were killed by a human vessel possessed by the spirit of the Alva'ci. Another died last night in a landslide that occurred after the widespread earthquakes across the world."

"I'm guessing then that five of us isn't a good number?" Mackenzie deduced aloud.

"Again, you are correct," Armond informed them. "There must be at least six agents of fate alive at all points in time for the spell to remain strong enough to keep the Alva'ci in its comatose state. Normally this wouldn't be a problem, statistically speaking, but there is a wildcard in play. With only five of you, the spell is breaking."

"What wildcard?" asked Shaun.

"The other agent of fate that isn't here," Armond continued. "His name is Hayden. There are very old prophecies concerning the eventual appearance of what was termed the 'cognizant one.' At a certain point in their life, this person would begin to absorb the powers of any other agent that died. Obviously, this creates a problem because those powers could not be passed on to new holders, and the concentration of several powers in one person does not behave in the same way as if they were spread amongst several people. The cognizant one from the prophecies is Hayden. With the spell breaking as it is, the Alva'ci will soon awaken and rise in another attempt to destroy humanity."

"Wait, so just thinking outside the box here for a second," Shaun interrupted. "What if we just sacrificed this Hayden guy? Like for the greater good and all… if he were to die right now, wouldn't all those powers go to new people and the spell go back into place?"

The suggestion drew some surprised gasps from around the room. Armond's expression turned stern.

"Firstly, Shaun," Armond began addressing the idea. "I fear the spell is already too weak for that to work. Secondly, I would never condone or allow the killing of one of our own. Finally, Hayden is far too strong and adept in the use of his powers already for you to even attempt it. The only way you will win this fight is as a team."

Shaun shook his head in acknowledgment. Mackenzie immediately posed another question to Armond. "So why isn't Hayden here?"

"Hayden defeated the possessed human vessel that I mentioned previously and stopped her from killing any more of the agents," Armond informed her. "But during the fight, he was stabbed. He is currently recovering from the effects of that injury."

"Will he be ready to fight if this Alva'ci thing shows up soon?" Mackenzie continued to inquire.

"I will make sure that he is ready," Armond answered her.

"So what do we do now?" Lora asked.

"Well, we've gone over the how and why already," Armond said to the group. "Now we can explore the basics of your powers, and I will teach you how to channel them and use them."

"So, like the fun part…" Shaun said excitedly.

"I suppose at first," Armond replied. "But we must concentrate, and you all must keep in mind that you will need these powers very soon to fight with. Your lives will depend on it. The lives of everyone on this planet will depend on it."

A more somber tone of realization swept the room with Armond's reminder to them. After a few moments of silence, Armond stood and asked the group to follow him to the backyard to test their powers. The group gathered on the lawn and waited for Armond's instructions.

"So, since none of you know what your power actually is yet," Armond addressed the group. "I will teach you to manifest it, and we can go from there. The easiest way to do this will be to close your eyes and concentrate on the thought and feeling of power deep inside you."

The group followed Armond's advice and stood silently, concentrating. After a few minutes, Lora gasped as she opened her eyes. She could feel the latent power in her beginning to rise. The back of her hand began to glow with the outline of a symbol. The rest of the group stared on in amazement at what was happening to her. Armond walked up to Lora and examined her hand.

"That symbol on your hand," Armond told her. "Is the word for Earth. You possess the power to control the soil, rocks, plants, and other things related to the physical planet."

The rest of the group refocused on manifesting their powers. Now that Lora had accomplished her goal, the inspiration given to them led to much quicker results.

"Shaun," Armond said as his hand lit with a symbol. "You have power over Water."

Just as they had arrived at the house together, Mackenzie and Tiffany's hands lit with their symbols at the same time.

Armond addressed them both. "Mackenzie, you have the power of Shadow. Tiffany, your power differs from the others, which I'm sure you now realize. Instead of an elemental or sub-elemental power, you possess the ability to cast the seven ancient spells. To do so, you must only recite the words of the spell. They are:

Abarus, which summons ethereal spirits that will aid you in battle.

Tithethus, which binds your opponent with vines.

Emiratus, which you can use to amplify the powers of the other agents of fate.

Prophesch'naya Con'di Ashante, which temporarily impairs the vision of your opponent.

Chantiatus, which will form a protective forcefield around you. If you become adept with this spell, you can also use it to protect others.

Youlvasius, which increases the accuracy of your attacks.

Amal Esta Preavius, which can summon several portals of energy. If the other agents direct their powers into these portals, their attacks will multiply against your opponent."

"Wow," Tiffany replied. "That's a lot."

"Yes, but the spells will come naturally to you now that you've heard them," Armond told her. "As I'm sure you've deduced, many of the spells allow you to support the team and make it easier for you to win as a group."

With the revelation of everyone's powers, the group had a renewed energy. Armond stayed up with everyone until dawn, experimenting with their new powers and learning how to control them.

ര ര ര ര ര ര

After sleeping for a couple of hours, the group tiredly reassembled in the dining room, where Armond made them a small meal. After he had prepared the food, Armond took a moment to check in with Kali and Dan on Hayden's status.

"Well, I suppose that no news is good news," Armond said to Kali over the phone. "Just let me know as soon as he wakes up."

Armond joined the others at the table and ate as the group enjoyed some friendly banter, now more relaxed with each other. As Tiffany and Lora were helping Armond clear the table after the meal, the television came to life with the high-pitched warning of the Emergency Alert System.

"This is not a warning. Hold for a message from the governor," the robotic alert voice stated.

Everyone fell silent and gathered in the living room to wait for the pending announcement. Soon an image of the capital flashed onto the screen, the governor standing at a podium with a concerned look on his face.

"Citizens of California," he began. "I've been given information that strange occurrences are happening in the vicinity of Yosemite National Park. Our scientists have noted strong electromagnetic disturbances coming from the area, along with continuous seismic activity. A mandatory evacuation order is in effect for the Yosemite Valley and all towns and cities within a fifty-mile radius of the Park. When evacuating, please do so in a path that immediately takes you away from this fifty-mile radius. More information will be provided as we know it."

The television returned to the daytime talk show that had previously been filling the room with background noise.

"What does…" Mackenzie began to ask.

A sharp jolt shook the ground, causing everyone to stumble, followed by another tremor that rolled on for two minutes.

"This is why I never wanted to live in California," Shaun joked.

"These are no normal earthquakes, I'm afraid," Armond responded. "Yosemite is where Hayden was stabbed after he fought the human vessel of the Alva'ci's spirit."

"So something big is going down there?" Tiffany concluded.

"Yes," Armond agreed. "The spell on the Alva'ci is almost gone. It is only a matter of time before it emerges. You should all travel up to Yosemite right now and get prepared.

Focus on practicing with your powers until I arrive."

"What about Hayden?" Lora asked.

"I am going to his apartment now to get him, and we will meet you all there," Armond replied.

"...but what if this Alva'ci thing shows up before you do?" Lora followed up.

"If that happens, you will know what to do," Armond admonished her. "Just let the powers inside all of you guide your minds and efforts."

The instructions were not as reassuring as Armond had hoped, and he could see it on the group's faces. Nevertheless, the four of them packed up some essentials and began making the drive to Yosemite.

Armond arrived at Hayden's apartment. Kali opened the door and let him in as she hung up the phone with Abby.

"Abby said that she got a little delayed over at Samantha's place and that she'll be here in the afternoon," Kali called out to Dan, who was still sitting in the front room with Hayden.

Armond walked into the front room and observed Hayden, who remained locked in an unwilling slumber on the couch.

"I fear that the time has come," Armond told them. "The Alva'ci is about to emerge. We need Hayden in this fight if we want any chance of winning."

"We've been watching him," Dan said. "And there's no change other than it looks like he's having some intense dream. His eyelids are moving all over, and occasionally he moves a little."

"Kali, go sit next to Hayden," Armond suggested. "Talk to him, say his name, touch him. Concentrate on speaking to him like you are speaking directly with his mind."

She did as Armond asked and sat next to Hayden on the couch, placing one hand on his arm and another on his cheek. She drew her face down near Hayden's and whispered his name again and again, pleading with him to wake up. After a minute with no changes, she closed her eyes and spoke to Hayden within her own head. She recounted their trip to Boston together and what it meant to her that Hayden took her with him. She continued recalling memories of her and Hayden together and told him about the moments within those memories that she cherished.

"Fight this, Hayden," she whispered as one of the tears that had been welling in her eyes fell onto Hayden's cheek. "I need you. We need you to fight this and come out of this dream. I love you."

Kali then began to recount to Hayden the memory that embodied the moment she knew she had fallen in love with him. Without warning, Hayden's body spasmed sudden-ly. Kali opened her eyes and jumped back, startled by the movement. Hayden's eyes were still closed, but he had moved. After seeing the first semblance of progress, Armond begged her to continue speaking to him.

～ ～ ～ ～ ～ ～

Hayden sat in the stone chair, exhausted and mentally drained after his encounter with the orb. He weighed the options that had been presented to him in his mind, all the while attempt-ing to remember that he was most likely being manipulated to some degree. He thought it unlikely that such an evil en-tity would let him and Kali live after wiping out the rest of humanity. Hayden concluded that this was most likely a ploy to make it easier for the Alva'ci to win by having Hayden take himself out of the equation.

"Besides," he thought to himself. "That orb did say that I had no idea of my own powers. It must fear what I can do if I knew my own potential."

In a moment, the darkness surrounding Hayden was flooded with an all-encompassing light. It penetrated ev-ery crevice of the dreamscape-induced land with swathes of golden daylight and was accompanied by an overwhelming feeling of warmth. Hayden felt the dread and chill in his bones momentarily change to hope as he suddenly thought of Kali. The light faded, and Hayden was back in the same scene as before.

Hayden remembered what he was fighting for as his mind was flooded with thoughts of moments that he and Kali had shared together. He stood up from the cold stone chair and began to approach the staircase in front of him.

"You say if I give up now, I live," Hayden called out to the orb.

"Correct," the orb simply stated.

"Where will I go then," Hayden inquired. "I assume you want this planet for yourself. Where will Kali and I go if you let us live?"

"We can come to an arrangement," the orb insisted. "I may have use for you."

"Because of my powers?" Hayden asked.

"Yes," again the orb suspiciously responded with a single word.

"But you said that I don't even know my own powers?" Hayden began to dig deeper. "What use would you have if I don't even know how to use my powers?"

"I know the full potential of your powers," the orb responded. "I had seen them when they were wielded by the most powerful users among humans. Even though they were no match for my strength, they were impressive nonetheless."

Hayden ascended the staircase and stood in front of the cage containing the orb. Suddenly he heard Kali's voice calling out his name as if she were speaking to him from across an abyss. He gazed into the cage at the bright orange light emanating from the orb.

"This place, this dreamscape as you called it," Hayden began to pry. "This is part of my power? So we are inside my head?"

"We are not inside your head," the orb insisted. "We are in a construct that can defy the rules of time and space. It is a place that your power alone can control to make it whatever you want it to be. We are here now because I am controlling your power."

Hayden was beginning to understand where he thought he could hold the advantage in the situation. He carefully pondered his next steps before continuing to speak.

"Can we die in here?" Hayden asked the orb.

"You cannot die within the dreamscape," the orb responded. "This place is fueled by your own powers. I could summon a firing squad at the bottom of that staircase to shred you with thousands of rounds of ammunition, and it would not harm you in reality. Your real body is vulnerable, though. That girl of yours could stab you in the neck right now in the real world, and you would die. You can kill others within the dreamscape, bringing them inside with you and mangling their minds so horrifically that it would leave them braindead in the real world. If you knew the true power of this construct, you could use it to control the minds of others outside by using its inherent power to push your thoughts and will into their mind."

"So you could die here?" Hayden baited.

"I cannot die here, and you would be foolish to think so," the orb replied. "The part of me that is in here with you is but a small sliver of my being. This orb-like appearance is a manifestation within the construct of the shard that is embedded in your side. It is nothing of my true nature and power."

Hayden stopped and thought, considering everything that the orb had told him. He focused his thoughts for a few moments and looked into the distance to see a bird appear out of nothingness, flying past him and into the endless void of grey fields at the edge of the room.

"You are trying to use your powers to escape this place?" the orb insinuated.

"No," Hayden replied. "I'm not going anywhere yet."

Hayden placed one hand on the bars of the cage in

front of him and raised his other hand into the sky. A stream of purple-tinged lightning erupted from the nothingness above him and flowed into his hand. The bars of the cage shattered into dust before him. Hayden placed both of his hands on the glowing orb.

 భ భ భ భ భ భ

Lora, Mackenzie, Tiffany, and Shaun arrived in Fresno, making a quick stop to fuel their car and grab some food. They had made exceedingly quick time due to the fact that no one was heading toward the city, and the highway patrol was entirely too busy with emergency response to be patrolling the freeways for speeding. The city was all but deserted. Though it was just outside the fifty-mile evacuation radius, most of the citizens had preemptively fled the area due to the steady stream of earthquakes rattling the entire region. After they rested for fifteen minutes, they made the remainder of the drive in just over thirty minutes with help from Shaun's lead foot.

The group arrived at the gates of the national park just after noon to find an eerie silence sweeping over the valley. No human or animal life was anywhere to be seen. The roads were littered with debris and rocks from the continuous tremors, though still mostly passable. A few miles past the entrance gates, they switched to traveling by foot when they encountered a portion of the road that was completely covered by a group of fallen trees.

"What do we do now?" Tiffany asked aloud to the others. "Where do we go?"

"I can feel a disturbance in the ground," Lora responded. "It must be my power. There's a strong magnetic field off in the distance. I think I can tell where it is coming from."

"Well then, lead the way," Shaun told her.

The group continued on into the park, taking in the scenery that, in normal circumstances, they would have stopped to enjoy. The sky began to darken as ominous clouds moved in from the east and covered the park, emitting numerous flashes of lightning and deep rolling thunder.

Once they arrived at the location that Lora felt, they looked around and found a peculiar scene. The ground was rattling beneath them, and rocks and twigs were floating just above the surface of the earth. They all exchanged concerned looks and continued to examine the surroundings.

"What do we do now?" Mackenzie asked the group.

"I guess all we can do is wait," Shaun replied. "Maybe we should all practice using our powers or something."

"That's probably a good idea," Tiffany said. "I would

like to try out some of these spells and see how I can use them to help all of you."

"Good idea," Shaun told her. "Let's all get as good as we can in whatever amount of time we have."

ↄ ↄ ↄ ↄ ↄ ↄ

As Hayden's hands touched the orb, he felt an overwhelming surge of power flowing through him. His mind felt as if it had been opened to infinite possibilities. The dark skies above him became riddled with flashes of lightning and columns of fire. The air surrounding the staircase blew with gale force.

"What do you hope to achieve?" mocked the orb.

"Everything," Hayden said simply.

Hayden closed his eyes and concentrated on the true knowledge of his powers. The glow of the orb crackled and pulsed with a fierce intensity as Hayden pushed his hands deeper within its sphere. Hayden felt more alive and aware than he ever had before.

"I can see them," Hayden spoke aloud to the orb.

"Those piteous fools that stand above me?" the orb responded. "They know not what is coming… you shall watch them all die as I mercilessly rip their bones from their flesh and enjoy their final torturous screams."

Hayden thrust his hands further into the orb. The wind whipping around him grew ever more fierce, and lightning struck all around the staircase. The expansive fields of grey bordering the room that held the staircase flickered and disappeared.

"I don't know them," Hayden replied to the orb, referencing the other four agents of fate. "I don't care about them."

"Good," the orb said. "You should care about none of the inferior humans that plague this planet."

Hayden grasped the orb in his hand and held it above his head, slowly clenching his fist around it. He drew in the knowledge and power that the orb contained and closed his fist, shattering the orb.

"I care less about you," Hayden said as the last wisps of light that had been the orb vanished.

Hayden's body emanated a bright orange glow as he descended from the staircase. He could physically feel the intensity of the new power flowing through his body. His mind had been opened to the true depth of possibilities embodied within him. He was able to draw additional energy from the shard lodged in his side. As he reached the last step of the staircase, he closed his eyes.

When Hayden opened his eyes, it was to Kali sitting beside him on the couch in his apartment. He gasped for air as if he were breathing for the first time.

"Oh, my God!" Kali screamed in a mixture of surprise and delight. "You're awake!"

Kali squeezed Hayden's body in a hug as he sat up. Dan and Armond stared on in shock at the sudden change in his condition.

"What happened, Hayden," Armond asked. "Where were you?"

"Learning," Hayden replied in a monotone voice. "Gaining my true potential."

"The effects of the shard had you trapped in a dream?" Armond continued to inquire.

"The dreamscape," Hayden said. "The Alva'ci underestimated me, and I used its mistake to enhance myself."

"That is a dangerous game to play, Hayden," Armond said in a decidedly worried tone. "That shard of rock is made up of the stone that comprises the Alva'ci's armor… but that armor is also a part of its being. Therefore, any power drawn from that shard has the potential to corrupt a person."

Hayden stood up from the couch and held his hand out towards the kitchen. The window that had previously cracked from the earthquake shattered into thousands of pieces and then floated across the room, hovering over Hayden's hand. Miniscule currents of electricity flowed in between the tiny fragments of glass as they continued to float in the air.

"Whoa," Dan said in shock at what he was witnessing.

In an instant, the glass flew back across the room to the kitchen, and the window reformed inside the pane. The crack was gone, and the window glistened as if it were brand new.

"Holy shit," Dan added to his previous statement as Armond and Kali looked on, speechless and amazed. Hayden turned to Kali.

"You spoke to me across the abyss of the dreamscape?" he asked her.

"I was talking to you when you were asleep, yeah," Kali stumbled on her words. "I was trying to wake you up any way that I could."

"Your memories," Hayden started. "I felt your memories. The one when you fell in love with me."

"You did?"

"It snapped me out of almost admitting defeat," Hayden continued. "It helped me become this."

"What is… this?" Armond asked cautiously.

Hayden walked to the front door and flung it open. The others followed him as he walked outside onto the front lawn.

"This is everything," Hayden's voice boomed. "I am

the pinnacle of power."

The shard began to glow with greater intensity as Hayden raised his arms up to the sky. Kali, Dan, and Armond looked on in wonder and a growing feeling of fear as the skies became blanketed with dark clouds. Lightning began to stream down across the city like rain.

"Why didn't you teach me this, Armond?" Hayden asked.

Armond attempted to speak but could only emit broken mumbles as he watched the landscape grow ever more dark. The group's fear now grew exponentially as they observed Dan and Armond's cars begin to float a few inches above their parking spots in the driveway.

"Hayden, what are you doing?" Kali called out to him in a panicked voice.

Hayden dropped his hands from the sky and turned back towards her. Instantaneously, the sky cleared of clouds and back to the sunny day that it had been when they walked outside. The previously levitating cars fell back to the pavement. Dan's wide-open eyes said what everyone couldn't quite vocalize.

"You made this possible, Kali," Hayden said as he walked up to her. "Thank you for reminding me what it is I am fighting for."

"Speaking of that, Hayden," Armond interrupted, now able to formulate a sentence albeit shakily. "The others need you in Yosemite."

Hayden didn't acknowledge Armond's words. He placed his hand on Kali's shoulder and looked into her eyes.

"My love," he softly said to her.

Kali and Hayden's bodies fell to the grass.

"What the fuck?!" Dan exclaimed in surprise and posed a question to Armond at the same time.

"Hayden just pulled Kali into the dreamscape," Armond somberly told him.

"What the hell does that even mean," Dan's voice still pitched with worry.

"It's another sphere of existence that Hayden can project himself and anyone else that he wishes into," Armond began to explain. "It's like a separate world that Hayden can create and change at a whim. I've read about it before, but it didn't seem particularly useful for him to know about as far as fighting the Alva'ci."

"Well, he definitely learned about it while he was out cold earlier," Dan said.

"Yes, it would appear he learned many things," Armond mused aloud. "But unfortunately, from a source that is only intent on corruption and destruction. The way he is acting right now is indicative of that shard's ability to corrupt a person's mind."

"How are we going to snap them out of it this time?" Dan asked.

"I'm going to try to reach Hayden telepathically," Armond told him. "Try to draw him back. I wasn't able to last time because it was the Alva'ci controlling the dreamscape using Hayden's power, so I was locked out. He should be able to hear me this time as long as he doesn't ignore me."

Armond knelt down in the grass next to Hayden and Kali and concentrated his mind on speaking to Hayden.

ღ ღ ღ ღ ღ ღ

Lora was practicing her powers by projecting fragments of rocks against a nearby cliffside when she was stopped dead in her tracks by an enormous jolt in the ground that threw her off her feet. Lora and the others looked at each other with palpable tension and a feeling of fear.

"What was that?" Tiffany asked, even though she knew that no one had the answer.

The air went frighteningly still around the group, and the earth stopped shaking.

"Where's Armond and Hayden?" Shaun asked in an

annoyed tone. "They should be here by now."

Boulders and trees began to disappear into the ground as the earth sank beneath them. They were soon replaced by eruptions of fire and smoke that burst up into the sky. Though they attempted to exhibit confidence, the feeling of fear within the group was observably growing with the changing landscape.

"This isn't good," Mackenzie mumbled as she watched.

The earth began to rumble again, the treeline near them dissipating as more trees fell to the ground. An ominous hum filled the air for minutes as lightning struck the mountains and hillsides all around the group.

"What do we do?" asked Tiffany.

No one had a chance to respond. Several hundred yards in front of them, the ground split open into a gaping crevice. Smoke billowed from the tear in the Earth's crust and into the already dark sky. An ear-piercing shriek permeated the air as the group stood frozen in place, looking at the crevice.

"Oh my God," Tiffany said, fear now wracking her voice.

A bright orange glow radiated from the crevice as a figure appeared on the edge before them, walking through the smoke and into their field of vision.

"Come to sacrifice yourselves to me?" boomed the menacing voice of the figure across the distance between them.

In a blinding flash of orange, the figure disappeared and reappeared, standing only twenty feet before them. Shaun's hands started to glow with the symbol of Water, and he began the fight without a word, sending an enormous column of liquid hurtling toward the Alva'ci. Lora and Mackenzie followed Shaun's lead and used their powers to join in on the attack. The Alva'ci easily deflected the incoming attacks and left the group stunned.

"What the fuck?" Shaun uttered in disbelief.

"My turn," the Alva'ci smugly said to the group.

Tiffany's instincts kicked in as the Alva'ci raised a hand toward them. "Chantiatus," she screamed, raising translucent forcefields around each member of the group. The Alva'ci blasted the barriers with an awe-inducingly powerful blast. The creature walked closer to the group after the forcefields proved to hold up.

"Let's go for a ride," the Alva'ci snarled.

The creature raised his hand again, and the group was thrown through the air over the mountains surrounding them. They landed with a hard thud against the ground on an island in the middle of Mono Lake, thirty-eight miles from where they had been standing. As they hit the ground, the forcefields finally gave out. The Alva'ci appeared in the sky above them and floated down, hovering about fifteen feet above the group.

"Do you think that those forcefields will protect you forever?" the Alva'ci said mockingly.

As the creature once again raised its hands to attack, Tiffany uttered the spell to restore the protective barriers around the group. They were still able to feel the intense heat as the Alva'ci blasted the land and water all around them. Mono Lake was vaporized in an instant, and they found themselves now standing on a hill in the middle of a dry lakebed.

ↄ ↄ ↄ ↄ ↄ ↄ

Kali looked around and found herself in the middle of a carnival. Her surroundings reminded her of a memory. Hayden came running up behind her and lifted her off the ground in a hug.

"Is this what I think it is?" she asked Hayden.

"It's where we first fell in love," he replied, his smile beaming. "It's just like the memory that you reached out to me with."

Kali looked on in amazement. She walked over to a

nearby booth and grabbed a stick of cotton candy from the attendant.

"It's real," she said with wonder in her voice as she brought it to her mouth. "I can taste it."

Hayden grabbed Kali by the hand and ran with her through the fairgrounds, arriving at the Ferris wheel.

"Do you remember?" he asked her.

"I do," she told him, recalling in her mind the place where Hayden had first kissed her years ago.

The two boarded the Ferris wheel, and the attendant started the ride. Kali and Hayden looked at each other and then into the skies as the stars glimmered with an almost unreal brightness. Kali nestled herself against Hayden, feeling the warmth from his body permeating hers.

"This is perfect," she told him.

In parallel with the night they spent together years prior, Hayden kissed Kali. She savored every moment as she recalled the memory in her mind. This time, however, she thought she wouldn't make the mistake of running away from their relationship.

"Stay with me, Kali…" Hayden asked her. "Forever?"

"Yes, I will, babe," she replied as she kissed him again.

The Ferris wheel arrived back at the loading station, and they disembarked. Hayden led Kali to a row of game booths and watched her as she played the various games of chance; however, always winning since Hayden was in control of the scene.

As they departed the game booths and walked hand-in-hand down the path, Kali took a moment to pause as she pondered something.

"Babe, if we're going to be together forever," she started. "Don't we need a world to live in?"

As she asked her question, Hayden's concentration on the dreamscape faltered long enough for him to hear Armond calling out to him telepathically. He stood in front of Kali and took both of her hands in his.

"Yes, you're right," he told her. "As much as I desire to just stay in this memory with you, I need to make the real world safe for us."

Hayden touched Kali's forehead, and the carnival disappeared in an instant. The couple awoke, still lying in the grass in front of Hayden's apartment, with Dan and Armond hovering over them.

"You're back!" Dan exclaimed.

Hayden stood up and helped Kali up from the ground as well.

"The Alva'ci has emerged," Armond told Hayden. "I can feel it. We must leave immediately and drive to Yosemite if it's not already too late."

"I know what I need to do," Hayden told Armond, his attitude still conveying his newfound sense of power. "You need to stay here and keep Kali and Dan safe."

"You're going to drive there all alone?" Kali asked Hayden.

"No," Hayden responded and kissed her on the lips. "I'm not driving anywhere."

Hayden stepped back from Kali, and his hands began to glow. Kali and the others looked on in wonder as Hayden's feet left the ground, and he began to levitate above the surface of the lawn.

"I love you, Kali," he told her. "I'll be back after I end this."

Hayden quickly rose into the sky, the airflow that emanated from his departure setting off car alarms and shaking nearby trees. After he ascended, Hayden streaked northward across the sky towards Yosemite. As he passed low over Brea and then the San Gabriel Valley, the shockwave from his wake shattered windows and rattled buildings.

"So, he can fly now also?" Dan asked the other two.

"Apparently so," Kali responded.

نوبات

Chapter Nine

The Gates of Hell

Tiffany steadied her stance and yelled. "Tithethus!"

Glowing vines of energy erupted from the hillside and pulled the Alva'ci down to the ground in front of the group. Immediately, the creature began to fight against the choking embrace of the vines.

"Emiratus, Youlvasius," Tiffany added to amplify the powers of the others.

Shaun, Mackenzie, and Lora followed by blasting the Alva'ci with their respective powers. They were encouraged to see that their attacks had landed this time. The Alva'ci fell back to the ground as the magical vines let loose.

"Did we do it..." Mackenzie cautiously asked the

others. "Did we win?"

As the group noticed a growing rumble in the distance that resembled a rolling thunder, the Alva'ci slowly rose back to its feet.

"Win?" the Alva'ci mockingly said. "You didn't even scratch my armor."

As the thunderous sound in the sky grew even louder, the Alva'ci vanished in a bright orange flash and almost instantly reappeared behind Mackenzie. It fired off a blast of energy at her forcefield so powerful that the resulting shockwave threw Lora, Tiffany, and Shaun from their feet. Mackenzie's forcefield began to flicker and fade under the unrelenting attack of the Alva'ci.

The sound emanating from the sky was almost deafening now. On the horizon to the south, a glimmer of light twinkled like a newly born star.

The Alva'ci halted its energy attack as Mackenzie's forcefield failed. The others looked on in horror as the Alva'ci grabbed her and held her in the air.

"Tell me, does this feel like winning?" the Alva'ci snarled at her.

Mackenzie let out a haunting scream as the Alva'ci ripped one of her legs clean from her body and flung it across the lakebed. The object from the horizon now resembled a shooting star as it tore through the sky. The winds along the flat salt-drenched stretch of dirt whipped around like a tornado had just made landfall.

"Let her go!" Shaun demanded as he attempted to struggle to his feet. "I'll kill you!"

"I'll let her go," the Alva'ci sarcastically retorted.

Mackenzie's whimpers of pain couldn't be heard by the others over the howling wind. The Alva'ci looked menacingly into her eyes as the others attempted to stand again. The Alva'ci struck Mackenzie with its other fist, which pierced straight through the middle of her chest, shattering her sternum.

"Mackenzie, no!" Lora's voice faltered and cracked as she screamed out in horror.

The Alva'ci drew its fist downward and cut through Mackenzie's body, ultimately tearing a hole through her flesh from her chest to just above her right hip. The creature threw her body on the ground in front of Lora, Tiffany, and Shaun. They watched as copious amounts of blood spilled from her wounds and organs slid out onto the lakebed. Tiffany vomited all over the salt-dusted ground in front of her.

The shooting star-like object that was streaking across the sky stopped directly above the lakebed, and the resulting shockwave sent a cloud of dirt into the air for miles. Lora,

Tiffany, and Shaun looked up to see what appeared to be a human figure floating in the air above them.

"Another one comes to die," the Alva'ci said with a smirk on its face.

Hayden descended from the air above the scene, touching down next to the other agents of fate. He looked around and examined the field of battle and Mackenzie's nearby body, noting that the fight appeared to be going in favor of the Alva'ci so far. Hayden could feel wafts of power radiating from the creature.

"Are you Hayden?" Tiffany asked.

"I am," he responded matter-of-factly.

"We could've used you several minutes ago!" Shaun barked at him. "Mackenzie is dead now!"

Hayden appeared to pay no attention to what Shaun was saying to him. He stood in front of the others facing the Alva'ci, who disappeared and then reappeared a dozen feet away from the group.

"You've come to meet your end along with the others, Hayden?" the Alva'ci mocked as it pointed towards Mackenzie's body.

"Quite the contrary," Hayden coldly replied. "I've come to end you."

"Do you actually think that sliver of energy you may

have gained from that orb will do anything to help you?" asked the Alva'ci. "I tore through your companion's body like it was paper. You should have seen the fear on her face as she felt my hand shredding her insides. I will mutilate these other three in front of you so that you can see your failure, and then I will kill you. As your eyes dim to this world, your final thought will be your helplessness in knowing that I will be slowly and tortuously tearing apart the body of Kali next. I will savor every whimper and scream that she makes as she pleads for her life and then watch the blood pour from her mangled body. The rest of humanity's deaths will seem gracious compared to hers."

Hayden's expression turned to rage as he lifted his hands in the air at his sides. As the back of his hands cycled through the symbols of all the powers he had accumulated, the shard in his side began to glow brightly. Shaun, Lora, and Tiffany all noticed the strange glow and were instantly intrigued.

"What the hell is that?" Shaun yelled out to Hayden. "You're glowing the same color as that monster. What are you?"

Once again, Hayden ignored Shaun's question as the shard continued to glow brighter. He was still drunk with power, exhibiting the same attitude as he had with Armond back in Fullerton. Although he had defeated the orb inside the dreamscape and used the encounter to enhance his powers, the corruptive force of the Alva'ci resident within the orb still altered his behavior. Where he once could be described as a vestige of patience and empathy, he was now bordering on delusions of grandeur. Hayden clenched his fists and closed his eyes. An aura of pale blue light surrounded Lora, Tiffany, and Shaun and then floated through the air to Hayden. The symbols on Hayden's hands changed their pattern, which now also included the symbols that represented the powers of the other three agents. Shaun feared the worst had happened and that Hayden had left them all powerless. He tried to activate his power to no avail.

"He stole our powers!" Shaun cried out to Lora and Tiffany in disbelief and disgust. Not only did he feel entitled to an answer from Hayden, but he also felt extremely vulnerable without his only real means of protection.

Lora tried to activate her power to confirm what Shaun had speculated. She found that he was correct in his assumption. Visible waves of energy, unlike what the other three had ever seen before, started flowing forth from Hayden's body as he drew both hands in front of him and pointed in the direction of the Alva'ci.

The creature decided to strike first and sent a column of energy blasting toward Hayden. The others gasped at the sheer magnitude of the deadly wave of energy and prepared themselves for the devastating impact. With a flick of the wrist, Hayden deflected the blast and sent it into a nearby mountainside, leaving only a crater in the earth behind. The Alva'ci smirked at the results of its attack. Though it had failed to land a blow against Hayden, it recognized that he may actually present an entertaining challenge.

"I'm going to enjoy killing you!" the Alva'ci yelled out to Hayden.

Hayden's hands were now enveloped in crackling energy. He had reached levels of power that were far greater than what Armond had taught him. Hayden opened his hands with his palms facing the Alva'ci. Without uttering a word, an amplifying portal appeared directly in front of Hayden as if he had cast the spell Amal Esta Preavius. In an instant, a massive infusion of all the combined powers flowed from Hayden's palms and struck the Alva'ci. The staggering blast continued to flow uninterrupted, growing in intensity as Hayden focused all of his rage on the creature. Pieces of the Alva'ci's armor were visibly torn from its body and strewn across the lakebed. The others now watched with a returning glimmer of hope in their eyes and an awestruck mixture of fear and respect for Hayden's power.

Hayden's energy blast concluded. As the smoke

cleared from the impact zone, the Alva'ci was seen crumpled on the ground. As it attempted to rise up once again, Hayden pointed his hand out towards the unpopulated expanse of land behind the group. Lora, Tiffany, and Shaun all watched as the symbol of Earth lit the back of Hayden's hand. They had become used to seeing Lora use her power to hurtle rocks and small boulders through the air, but they were not prepared for what they witnessed next. The ground shook beneath them as one of the mountains behind them crumbled. Fragments of rock and debris the size of automobiles filled the air and came hurtling toward their location. As the objects approached, Hayden's hand lit with the symbol of Fire, and the airborne field of rock and debris lit ablaze.

Again, without actually saying the spell, Hayden brought up forcefields around himself and the others. The fiery stones screamed overhead the group and landed with an explosive detonation atop the Alva'ci. As the last rock impacted, Hayden's hand lit with the symbol of Electricity, and two unnaturally massive bolts of current cut through the sky and struck the Alva'ci. Its remaining scraps of armor fell to the ground beneath it as it struggled to stand back up.

Hayden paused for a moment when he felt Armond reaching out to him telepathically. His advisor and newfound friend pleaded with him to fight the corruption of the shard and pour his will into saving humanity. Hayden began to tune his mind away from the shard's influence and concentrate on ending the fight. He turned back to the others and waved his hand out in front of them. They were still frozen in a state of disbelief at what they had just seen. The auras of blue light returned, and Lora, Shaun, and Tiffany regained the ability to use their powers, though Hayden also retained the use of their powers. The Alva'ci stood and slowly walked towards the group.

"How is that thing not dead?" Tiffany asked.

"That part will take all of us together," Hayden answered. "Get ready to fight and be ready to use all of the spells at once."

Tiffany shook her head in acknowledgment. She began saying the words to all seven spells as Shaun, Lora, and Hayden activated their powers. As a group, they unleashed a barrage of attacks at the Alva'ci. They could see that the creature was now, in fact, taking on damage with its armor finally gone.

As it struggled to free an arm from the new set of vines holding it down, the Alva'ci was able to fire off a blast of energy. The group's forcefields were hit and disappeared from the blast. As Tiffany started to cast the spell again, the Alva'ci shot off another blast of energy in her direction. The pulse of energy struck Tiffany and sent her flying through the air. She landed on her back ten feet behind the others in the group and cried out in pain.

Shaun and Lora reacted by stopping their attacks and running over to Tiffany to help her. With only Hayden still casting his powers, the Alva'ci was able to deflect his incoming attack back at him. The impact on Hayden's forcefield sent him hurtling back in the air thirty feet. Hayden restored the forcefield just before hitting the ground, but he was still stunned by the collision.

Shaun and Lora knelt next to Tiffany and examined her injuries. The Alva'ci appeared behind them and struck them, swatting them both through the air like insects. As they stood back up and tried to run back to help Tiffany, the Alva'ci grabbed her by the leg and held her in the air. Tiffany pleaded for her life through her sobs as she feared what was coming. Lora and Shaun stood only a few feet in front of her, now petrified with fear.

In the distance, Hayden was slowly recovering and trying to return to his feet to launch a counterattack. However, he was not able to manage to do so in enough time. Lora and Shaun watched on, remorse in their eyes for Tiffany. The Alva'ci grasped at her other leg, piercing the skin near the ankle and wrapping its fingers around the bone. Tiffany cried out in pain as the Alva'ci yanked its hand upwards, pulling the tibia and fibula bones clean out of her leg, leaving the remaining muscle and skin dangling from her knee. Tiffany's cries turned to blood-chilling screams.

"Witness what will soon be your fates as well," the Alva'ci calmly said to Lora and Shaun, who watched on in terror.

The Alva'ci flung the bones onto the lakebed and drew its hand back above Tiffany, who was still dangling in the air by her one intact leg. The very little that was left of her tattered clothing was hanging from her body by its threads. The hand of the Alva'ci changed shape, the end of its finger now resembling a frighteningly sharp blade. Tiffany's screams had now turned into whimpers of somber realization that she was not going to survive this day. As she waited for the inevitable, Tiffany held a despondent gaze with Lora and Shaun.

The razor-sharp hand of the Alva'ci reached around Tiffany's body and pierced her skin just above her pubic bone. Tiffany couldn't hold back the involuntary screams of pain as the creature's blade-like hand sliced straight in through muscle and tendon, eventually perforating her uterus. Lora and Shaun watched as the Alva'ci then drew its hand down towards the ground, slicing through Tiffany's abdomen and chest until it withdrew its hand at her neck. Her previously labored breathing turned into a faint series of gurgling gasps before ceasing altogether. Tiffany's flesh sprawled open along the path traced through her body by the Alva'ci to reveal that it had cut straight through bone. Blood and organs poured from her body onto the ground, pooling in front of Shaun and Lora.

"Fuck," was all that Shaun could manage to feebly utter as the Alva'ci dropped what was left of Tiffany on the ground in front of them, causing the pooled blood to splatter onto them. Lora found that she could hardly think and definitely couldn't formulate any audible sound that resembled a word, her body and emotions in a state of shock from witnessing Tiffany's death.

The Alva'ci stood tall and menacing as it started to take steps towards them to levy similar fates. Lora and Shaun barely recognized what occurred in the ensuing blur of action. Hayden, now standing in the back of the Alva'ci, had his hands ablaze with the symbols of Lightning and Energy. As he swung his arms through the air, a blade of lightning formed in his hands and struck the side of the Alva'ci with a devastating blow. The creature flew through the air with immense speed, only stopping as it made an impact with the side of a mountain a couple miles away from the group. Shaun and Lora rose to their feet and walked over to Hayden.

"Is it finally dead?" Lora asked him.

"I don't know," Hayden responded.

As the cloud of dust and debris from the mountain cleared into the air, the three agents of fate saw a tiny shimmer of orange from the gaping hole left in the rock. Seconds later, the Alva'ci reappeared in front of them, though now visibly weakened and injured. Hayden closed his eyes and concentrated.

"Both of you cast your powers at me," Hayden directed.

Without questioning his methods, Shaun and Lora both activated their powers and fired them at Hayden. Hayden reached out one hand towards them and, with it, absorbed their blasts of Water and Earth. He extended his other hand out toward the sky, an energy portal appearing in front of his palm. A swirl of energy blasted into the portal and reappeared in the sky above the Alva'ci. A bedazzling pillar of infused power twenty feet in diameter rained down onto the Alva'ci. Pieces of earth flew out in all directions as the enormous blast of energy tore a crater into the ground and pierced the Alva'ci's flesh. As the blast of energy from Hayden ended, remnants of fire and smoke billowed from the chasm. The Alva'ci crawled over the cusp of the hole in the lakebed and stumbled to its feet, now struggling to maintain its footing.

"You may not die today, Hayden," the Alva'ci muttered. "But you will live to regret it."

Hayden readied himself to attack again. With a flick of its wrist, the Alva'ci opened a glowing orange portal of energy next to itself. The creature stepped into the portal and disappeared. Hayden let his guard down and spoke to the others.

"Are you two okay?" he asked Lora and Shaun.

"I think I'm forever going to be mentally scarred," Lora answered.

"But we're alive," Shaun offered.

"If we won the fight," Lora mused aloud. "Then why would we regret the day?"

"Fuck," Hayden said in a despondent voice, realizing what the Alva'ci meant by its cryptic threat. "I have to go. Get back to Fullerton as quickly as you can."

Before Lora or Shaun could protest or ask questions, Hayden was airborne, accelerating through the sky toward Orange County with blistering speed.

❧ ❧ ❧ ❧ ❧ ❧

Kali, Dan, and Armond were standing in the front yard of Hayden's apartment, waiting for any news and trying to remain hopeful that Hayden would be able to assist the other four agents and save the world.

"What I wouldn't give to go back in time a week and only have finals to worry about," Dan said, trying to keep the mood light instead of facing the feeling of dread that was confronting them all.

"I know the feeling, Dan," Kali responded. "I wish I hadn't wasted those years apart from Hayden. We could've spent all that time together if I hadn't been so selfish."

"Hey, don't be hard on yourself," Dan attempted to offer her some insight. "You don't know if things would've even worked out if you had stayed. Maybe that time apart is what made it ultimately possible for you to be together in the long run."

"Thanks, Dan. I appreciate you trying to make me feel better."

The group looked up as they heard a distant rumble. What looked like smoke from an enormous fire hundreds of miles away stained a portion of the northern sky.

"That's probably not good…" Dan said worriedly, "…right?"

A bright object appeared in the north from where the smoke was originating. It appeared to be moving closer to them at a very high rate of speed.

"That's gotta be Hayden," Dan's voice changed to an excited tone. "Maybe this is good!"

As the object neared their position, seventy-mile-per-hour winds whipped through the city. The winds ceased as quickly as they had originated when Hayden stopped in the air above them.

"It is him!" Dan exclaimed and waved at his friend. "He must have made it down here in like thirty seconds."

Hayden quickly descended to the ground, but as he touched down, he lost the sense of hope that he had briefly held as an orange portal appeared behind the others. Before Hayden could act, the Alva'ci stepped from the portal and grabbed Kali. Armond and Dan jumped back in a combination of surprise and horror at seeing the creature for the first time. Hayden stepped closer.

"If you hurt her," Hayden snarled at the Alva'ci. "I will draw out your death so excruciatingly long that you will pray for an end to it."

"Do you really think you can defeat me alone?" the Alva'ci mocked him. "You and your companions haven't succeeded thus far."

"You're badly injured," Hayden confidently responded. "I won't need the others here to bring an end to your life."

"Unfortunately, you won't get the chance to find out if

that's true or not," the Alva'ci told him.

Hayden's clenched fists began to glow intensely. "Let go of her and fight me!" he demanded, the rage building inside him unmistakable in his tone.

The Alva'ci raised one hand to its side and fired off a blast into the portal. A second portal opened directly behind Hayden, and the blast poured out from it, hitting Hayden squarely in the back. Hayden fell to the ground, and the Alva'ci stepped backward with Kali still clenched in its hand. As Hayden struggled to his hands and knees, the shard of orange rock fell from his side and rattled on the ground beneath him. Before Hayden could rise to his feet, the Alva'ci walked through the portal with Kali. Hayden lunged forward towards the portal, but it vanished before him.

Dan and Armond stood near Hayden in complete shock, at first unable to speak. Hayden began to frantically look around as if he would be able to find Kali anywhere nearby.

"Hayden…" Dan said shakily. "Where did it take her?"

"I don't know, Dan!" Hayden yelled in unfocused anger.

Hayden's will and strength left his body, and he fell to his knees on the lawn. His body began to visibly tremble with rage, and the skies grew dark above them. Armond looked around in growing distress. Hayden slammed his fists into the grass, and the ground began to shake throughout the city. Loose roof shingles and tree branches fell to the ground as the quake intensified, and lightning began to strike nearby power poles and buildings.

"Hey, buddy..." Dan said, trying to calm Hayden. "Let's get up and figure out a plan together."

"Dan is right," Armond finally spoke in agreement. "This isn't helping anything."

Hayden stood and walked towards his friends. The look of pure and unadulterated rage on his face was unlike anything Dan had ever seen in his friend.

"A plan?!" Hayden retorted. "There is no plan! The world may have won, but I lost."

Hayden raised his hand to the street behind him. "Fuck!" he screamed at the top of his lungs as he fired a blast of energy directly into a parked car, reducing it to little more than ashes on the pavement.

"Uhhhh..." was all Dan could manage to mutter as he looked onward at the embers that used to be an automobile.

Hayden did not appear to be calming down even after his destructive outburst. Armond's cell phone rang in his pocket. He slowly looked at the screen to see Abby calling him. He answered the phone on speaker while still looking

Hayden dead in the eyes.

"It's really not a good time, Abby," he told her.

"You need to turn on the news, Armond!" she urged him. "They're talking about Hayden and showing videos of unbelievable things up north."

"Okay," Armond said to patronize her. "I've got to go for now."

Armond hung up the phone and shrugged at Hayden. Dan's gaze turned from the car to the ground in front of him.

"Dude, isn't that the shard of rock that was in your side?" Dan asked. "Do you think you can use that to find Kali?"

Hayden seemed to snap out of his rage-filled trance. He looked back at the shard. Hayden had hardly noticed that it had become dislodged during all the panic. He picked it up from the ground and closed his fist around it. The shard glowed orange, and Hayden felt his power growing, but he could not sense Kali.

"It may be the answer, Dan," Hayden told him. "But I don't think it's going to be easy to get that answer. I'm sorry for directing my anger at you guys."

"It's understandable, given the situation. Let's go inside and figure out what Abby was talking about," Armond begged Hayden. Dan's body language indicated that he concurred with Armond's statement.

With a nod, Hayden agreed, and the three of them walked inside his apartment. Armond switched on the television to a news channel. Grainy and jerky cell phone video footage filmed from somewhere near Mono Lake was playing on the screen. The news anchors rambled on in disbelief as they attempted to explain what was playing out over the airwaves. From a distance, the video showed several explosions, the volleys of attacks between the agents of fate and the Alva'ci, and even the mountainside being destroyed by the impact of the creature after Hayden had sent it flying through the air.

"That was a badass move," Dan told Hayden.

"Thanks," Hayden replied. "I was getting it back for slicing Tiffany in two."

Armond sighed as Hayden coldly relayed the news of Tiffany's death.

"Are the other three…?" Armond began to ask.

"Lora and Shaun are beat up, but okay," Hayden replied. "Mackenzie is dead."

The images on the television changed to a reporter in the town of June Lake. He was standing outside one of the local stores with two blood-soaked individuals.

"Looks like Shaun and Lora didn't make it too far

before they found themselves on television," Hayden said, annoyed.

Shaun briefly explained what happened at the lakebed and mentioned Hayden, Lora, and himself by name. The reporter admitted that she probably wouldn't have believed their story if it wasn't for the cell phone video footage showing all of the extraordinary events.

"That guy is a little bit of an ass if you ask me," Hayden said in reference to Shaun.

The next portion of the newscast showed footage of the scene from a news helicopter that had already made its way to the area. The camera scanned the lakebed and the surrounding landscape, including the crevice inside Yosemite National Park where the Alva'ci had emerged.

"As you can see in this unbelievable live footage," the news anchor said. "Mono Lake has been completely emptied of water. A portion of Yosemite National Park shows a large hole in the Earth's crust that scientists are speculating is the result of seismic activity that has been plaguing the park over the last day and prompted the governor's evacuation order earlier this morning. Near Mono Lake, two mountains have been completely destroyed and another decimated by an impact that caused a massive crater in its side. If the cell phone footage and eyewitness accounts are to be believed, this destruction was caused during a fight between an alien crea-ture and up to five superpowered humans."

The helicopter footage panned across the lakebed but quickly cut away as it came across the pools of dried blood and the bodies of Mackenzie and Tiffany.

"I'm deeply sorry for showing that," the news anchor frantically said. "Our helicopter pilot has cut back and will no longer show any footage of the lakebed until after first responders have had the chance to make it to the scene. Our reporter in June Lake has just told our newsroom staff that the person she was interviewing, Shaun Brooks, confirmed that two of the humans that were on the lakebed with him and Lora Parsons were, in fact, killed by the alleged alien lifeform. Their names were Mackenzie Beckham and Tiffany Woolf. Also accompanying Parsons and Brooks was Fullerton resident Hayden de Vere, whom Lora Parsons described as instrumental in the fight but is no longer in the area. We will update you if we receive more information on the partici-pants and what happened here today."

The newscast then devolved into a continuous loop of the same information coupled with speculative accounts from outside correspondents. Hayden turned off the televi-sion.

"Okay, well, that's enough of that," Hayden said. "So

much for keeping a low profile."

"Once the story gets straight though, people are going to see you as a hero," Dan told Hayden.

"Yeah, a hero that couldn't even protect those two girls that died on the lakebed or save his own girlfriend," Hayden said in a defeated tone.

"You'll find her, bro," Dan assured him.

The sound of several vehicles pulling up outside caught the attention of Hayden, Dan, and Armond. Hayden peeked through the curtains of the front window to see a group of news reporters and cameras piling out of several vans.

"Well, that was quick," Hayden scoffed. "I guess it's time to go take care of the inevitable."

Hayden flung the front door open, and Dan and Armond followed him into the front yard where the news teams had set up shop.

خاطِر

Chapter Ten

The Amulet

Hayden returned home from June Lake after flying back up to the area at the request of Armond. He had completed a plethora of tasks to clean up the wake of the fight with the Alva'ci, including burying the bodies of Mackenzie and Tiffany, filling in the crevice in the Yosemite Valley with the use of his powers, and creating an enormous supercell storm over Mono Lake that partially refilled it with unabated torrential downpours over the course of a week.

He sank into his pillow as he lay there exhausted and feeling defeated. As he scanned the room, Hayden saw a seemingly endless amount of reminders of Kali... her hairbrush and makeup on the nightstand, a picture of her and Hayden that she had framed and hung on the wall, and a liberal littering of shorts, tops, dresses, bras, and panties that had been left in various piles across the floor of the bedroom to be picked up later. He didn't want to move anything of Kali's in the hope that she would return to their apartment soon. As he lay still in the bed, lost in thought, he eventually decided that tomorrow he would at least pick up her dirty clothes and wash them. It was only 4:00 p.m., but Hayden fell asleep and didn't wake again until 10:00 a.m. the next morning.

Dan and Abby arrived at Hayden's apartment soon after he woke up and waited for Hayden in the living room while he took a shower. Abby tried to straighten up the main living area, but at the warning of Dan, made sure to leave anything of Kali's in its place.

Hayden walked down the hall from the bathroom and joined his friends. He hadn't bothered to style his barely dry hair, and his outfit reflected his less-than-stellar mood.

"Is there anything I can do for you?" Abby asked Hayden.

"You don't have to," he told her.

"C'mon, maybe I can make us all some food?" Abby insisted on helping out.

"Yeah, I suppose," Hayden replied. "I guess I haven't eaten in a day or two."

Dan looked at Abby, and the two shared a look of

concern about their friend's state. Abby headed into the kitchen and looked through the fridge for something she could make a meal out of.

Dan followed Hayden as he walked down the hallway to his bedroom. Hayden began to pick up Kali's assortment of clothing and undergarments from the floor and place them in a laundry basket. As Hayden neared the bed, he grabbed the last of Kali's clothes that she had removed next to it just before she and Hayden had sex the night before he got trapped in the dreamscape. He tossed everything into the laundry basket except for the shirt that Kali had been wearing that night. Hayden held it to his face and breathed in the smell of her perfume, which was still lingering on the fabric. Dan stood by silently, not quite knowing what to say to his friend at this moment. After a minute, Hayden placed the shirt on top of the laundry and walked back down the hallway to the laundry room. Dan watched him as he slowly and thoughtfully placed each piece into the washing machine.

Abby called out from across the room. "Lunch is done, guys!"

Hayden switched on the washer, and he and Dan joined Abby in the dining room.

"Kind of concerned about you, bro," Dan managed to reluctantly say as the group sat down for their meal.

"I'll be fine, Dan," Hayden unenthusiastically offered.

"Yeah, see, except that doesn't sound very convincing," Dan countered.

"Dan, I feel crippled by my inability to figure out how to save Kali," Hayden replied in an honest and shockingly earnest confession. "I feel lost without her here. What is the point of slogging through each day when I can't even use this insane amount of power that I have to accomplish the only goal that I care about right now?"

"Hayden, you're depressed…" Abby said in the softest tone she could manage, "…and that's alright to acknowledge. Anyone would be depressed after the trauma that you just went through. No matter what happens, though, we're here for you to help you get through it. Things will get better in time."

"I don't foresee it getting better if I don't find Kali," Hayden replied.

"Well, it's hard to see the end of the tunnel when you're lost in the darkness, but it's there," Abby offered.

Abby's words stung. Hayden knew those words all too well. He got up and walked to the kitchen, where he grabbed the shard from the counter and then sat back down at the dining room table with his friends. They watched as Hayden gripped the shard in his hand, and it began to glow.

He closed his eyes and concentrated for a minute while Dan and Abby waited in silence.

"All I can see is darkness," Hayden said angrily as he opened his eyes and tossed the shard onto the table.

The group sat in silence for several minutes until Dan hurriedly shared an idea that came to him. "What if the darkness is space? Wouldn't that make sense if the Alva'ci is an alien?"

Hayden looked at his friend with a bewildered expression, as if he wasn't sure if the random idea was worth considering or not. The more Hayden thought about it, the more it made sense.

"You could be on to something," he told Dan.

"I always held the belief that I'm the genius in our group," Dan said as he laughed aloud.

"Well, don't go claiming that title just yet…" Hayden replied as the buzzer on the washing machine went off.

Hayden stood from his seat and appeared to be in a slightly better mood than before hearing Dan's possible revelation. He walked to the laundry room and switched its contents to the dryer. After flicking the machine on, he walked through the dining room on his way to the bedroom.

"Nice wardrobe you have there," Dan now freely joked, seeing Hayden was in a better mood.

Hayden stopped for a moment and looked at his friend. Abby shook her head in secondhand embarrassment for Dan.

"These?" Hayden held up the several bras in his hand that he had taken from the washing machine. "You're not supposed to put bras in the dryer, dude, they're supposed to air dry, or they won't last as long."

Abby decided to pile on while she had the chance. "How do you not know that, Dan?" she joked. "At least Hayden knows how to take care of a woman."

"Wow," Dan replied to them sarcastically. "You guys are teaming up on me now. That's awesome."

"I'm just throwing out some facts for you, Dan," Abby continued while laughing. "A guy knowing how to properly launder a bra is much more attractive than him just knowing how to take one off of you."

I mean, if you manage to get both, though…" Hayden jokingly interjected.

"Oh, green flag all the way," Abby added.

"Well, now I know!" Dan said to them, clearly over the joke.

Hayden smirked as he continued down the hallway and hung Kali's bras to dry on a hanger near the bed. When he reemerged in the dining room, Abby made a suggestion to the group.

"Why don't we all go see a movie?" she asked.

Dan gave her a nod of approval and then looked to Hayden for his opinion.

"Yeah, I guess I'm down for that," Hayden replied, still slightly guarded in his mood.

The three of them set out to the movie theater and decided on a film to watch. Though Hayden attempted to remain engaged and enjoy himself, he found that his mind wandered several times during the movie in an attempt to figure out how he could manage to find Kali if she was somewhere out in space.

❧ ❧ ❧ ❧ ❧ ❧

The next morning Hayden woke and rolled out of bed, this time at 9:00 a.m. After using the bathroom and showering, he gathered Kali's bras that were still dangling from the hanger next to the bed and placed them in one of her dresser drawers with the others. Hayden walked down to the kitchen and grabbed a doughnut for a quick breakfast. Before he settled on the couch, he remembered that he hadn't taken the clothes out of the dryer from the day before. He restarted the dryer on the wrinkle release setting and watched television for fifteen minutes until they were done.

After hanging and putting away all of Kali's remaining clothes from the dryer, Hayden returned to the living room. He tuned out the television program and thought about finding Kali. Hayden grabbed the shard from the dining room table and returned to the couch to give his search another shot.

After thirty minutes of trying various methods of finding Kali using the shard, Hayden once again admitted defeat. He could feel the tinge of depression starting to seep back into his mind as he sat motionless on the couch. Instead of letting himself sink back into that mental state, he decided to do something about it.

Hayden laid down on the couch and mentally prepared himself for what he was about to do. Once he was relaxed, Hayden touched his fingers to his temple, and his body went limp.

A large open field of tall green flowing grasses, covered in sunlight, surrounded Hayden as he opened his eyes. It was quite possibly the most serene and welcoming place that Hayden had ever seen. He walked through the field, his hand at his side floating over the tips of the grass. As he proceeded, he approached a small hill that overlooked the expanse of the landscape.

Atop the hillside stood a girl in a flowing red knee-length dress that was blowing about with the breeze. She was gazing off into the field strewn out before her. Hayden walked up behind her and placed his arms around her waist. She turned to face him, and he kissed her.

"I've been waiting for you," Kali spoke to him after their kiss concluded.

"I won't make you wait ever again," Hayden told her.

Kali sank into his arms, and Hayden looked over the picturesque fields as he held her.

ೲ ೲ ೲ ೲ ೲ ೲ

Dan and Abby arrived at Hayden's apartment after they couldn't reach him on the phone for several hours. Since everyone in the group now had keys to each other's places, Dan opened the door after Hayden failed to answer after repeated knocks.

As the two friends entered Hayden's place, they were initially relieved to see him asleep on the couch. Dan walked over to Hayden and lightly shook him by the arm to wake him up. After no response, Dan tried again, this time more aggressively.

"Oh damn," Dan muttered as he realized that he had seen this before.

"What's wrong?" Abby asked him.

"He's in this like dreamscape thing," Dan answered. "Armond explained it as some type of alternate plane that Hayden can use to create these elaborate scenarios."

"Why would he be in there?" Abby inquired.

"My guess," Dan replied. "Is that he's with some imaginary version of Kali."

"Oh," Abby said with a look of consternation and concern.

Dan took his phone from his pocket and dialed Armond.

"We have a slight problem," he told Armond after he answered.

"What problem?" Armond asked.

"Hayden has put himself in that dreamscape thing," Dan told him.

"He did it to himself," Armond wondered aloud. "Why would he do that?"

"I'm thinking that since he can't find Kali, he's creating a fake version of her so he can cope," Dan again offered his theory.

"That, unfortunately, makes complete sense," Armond replied. "I'll be right over."

Fifteen minutes later, Armond walked through the

front door of Hayden's apartment and sat in the chair next to the couch.

"I'm going to try to reach him telepathically," Armond stated to Dan and Abby.

Armond closed his eyes and focused on Hayden. After several minutes of trying to reach out across the dreamscape, Hayden awoke abruptly.

"What?" Hayden brashly questioned the group.

"What are you doing, bro?" Dan answered Hayden's question with a question.

"Let's call it self-soothing," Hayden replied curtly.

"So you're in there with Kali?" Dan continued questioning him. "Or an imaginary version of her."

"So what if I am?" Hayden responded. "This morning, I felt like I'd rather be in there than out here sometimes."

"That's kind of dark, bro, not gonna lie," Dan somberly said to Hayden.

"Well, I tried what you said yesterday about looking in space and found nothing again," Hayden replied. "So unless anyone has more ideas, then I'm at a total loss."

"Space?" Armond mused. "Yes, the creature would have most likely taken her back to an old home planet or something. The shard that you have is made from the same material as the Alva'ci's armor. From some of the more modern texts about the agents of fate and the Alva'ci, it was suggested that the shard's material was not native to Earth. Using various tools, the texts theorized that it may be possible to find these other home planets by narrowing down the candidates to only those where the material is found."

"Can we do that?" Dan asked in amazement. "That information would have come in handy yesterday."

"We may be able to," Armond replied. "But it will take time, possibly months."

"Do it," Hayden said in a flat, definitive tone.

Armond nodded. "I'll get to work on securing what we need. I will need you to bring the shard over when I get all set up so that I can run an analysis on it."

Armond left the apartment and headed back to his place to review the texts. Dan and Abby stayed with Hayden for the remainder of the day to make sure that he was okay.

ᏒᎧ ᏒᎧ ᏒᎧ ᏒᎧ ᏒᎧ ᏒᎧ

THREE WEEKS LATER

Hayden arrived at Armond's home with the shard. Knowing that there was nothing else he could do but wait, Hayden had kept himself busy over the previous weeks by going out constantly with Dan and Abby.

Hayden handed the shard to Armond and sat down in a chair across from the makeshift workstation in his garage. Armond placed the shard into a chamber to obtain its properties.

"How have you been?" Armond asked Hayden to pass the time.

"Pretty good, all things considered," Hayden responded. "I've been spending a lot of time out to keep my mind in the right place."

"That's good. Hopefully, with what we find, you'll be able to locate Kali quickly and bring her home."

The machine beeped to indicate that it was finished with the analysis. Armond grabbed the shard from the chamber and handed it back to Hayden. He went to work typing on the laptop that sat next to the analysis chamber.

"So, the next part of this process is to use the shard's properties and scan all nearby galaxies for planets or objects that contain the mineral," Armond informed Hayden as he continued to type. "The program will generate a list of all such planets that it finds. Then it is up to you to use that list to try and locate Kali. Once we've located her, then we need a plan to bring her back."

"How long does this program take to generate the list?"

Hayden asked him.

"Well, that's a bit of good news actually," Armond said with a smile. "My original assumptions figured it would take about a month to generate the list, but Abby helped me re-write the program on this laptop, and now the new estimate is two weeks."

Hayden nodded. Though he didn't want to wait even that long for the list, he did admit to himself that it was a vast improvement over the alternative.

"Thank you, Armond," Hayden said. "Do you need me for anything else? I'm planning on meeting Dan and Abby soon to keep focused on positive things."

"You're welcome, Hayden," Armond replied. "And no, I've got everything covered here. I'll call you as soon as the program is done running."

Hayden left Armond's house and headed downtown to distract himself with dinner and drinks.

♋ ♋ ♋ ♋ ♋ ♋

TWO WEEKS LATER

Armond handed Hayden the list, and the group waited impatiently to see what the results of this endeavor would be.

"Two objects in this solar system with trace amounts?" Hayden asked, admittedly a little surprised.

"My guess," Armond speculated. "Is that the trace amounts are from the Alva'ci visiting other planets before coming to Earth. However, I could be completely wrong."

"Well, we'll start with these two," Hayden concluded. "Either we eliminate them early, or we luck out, and everything is relatively close to home."

"My thoughts exactly," Armond agreed.

Dan and Abby sat on the couch and waited for the exchange of words between Hayden and Armond to end so they could see some action.

Hayden took a seat on the couch next to Abby and read the first entry on the list, the planet Neptune. Hayden closed his eyes and grasped the shard in his hand. An hour later, Hayden opened his eyes.

"Well, that took longer than I expected," Hayden said. "No luck on entry number one. Let's move on to number two, Pluto."

Again, thoroughly scanning the object for any signs of life took Hayden about an hour. Once again, Hayden informed the group that there was nothing to be found.

"Damn, couldn't have just been simple," Dan proclaimed in a discouraged voice.

"How about one more for today?" Hayden asked the group. "I know this must be kind of boring for you guys, just sitting around for hours."

"It's okay, Hayden," Abby answered. "Let's do it!"

Hayden nodded his head and thanked Abby for her encouragement. The next object on the list that Hayden read was outside the solar system. Hayden closed his eyes and focused on the planet for several minutes.

"I can't visualize it," Hayden said, confused.

"Try the next one," Abby suggested.

Hayden read the next entry on the list, also a planet outside the solar system. After several more minutes of concentration, Hayden was frustrated to find that he encountered the same result as the previous planet.

"Once I try to go outside our solar system, I can't see anything," he said to Armond.

"I'm speculating that, unfortunately, maybe your powers only reach so far," Armond offered as a possible explanation.

"What am I supposed to do about the other thirty entries on this list then?" Hayden asked.

"I don't know yet," Armond conceded. "We will have to think of a plan. Perhaps we can find a way to amplify your powers even more. Let's regroup tomorrow?"

"That sounds good to me," Dan agreed. "I'm pretty beaten."

"If you don't mind, Hayden," Abby said. "I'll stay here and make some dinner for you and me."

"You don't have to do that," Hayden told her.

"It's no problem," she insisted. "I want to."

"Okay," Hayden agreed, noting that he could use the company after such an unsuccessful day.

Armond and Dan headed out to their respective homes, and Abby made her way into the kitchen. Hayden followed her and offered to help with preparing dinner, but she refused.

"Go sit down and rest," she told him. "All that searching must have been tiring."

Hayden relented and took a seat in the dining room, watching Abby move back and forth between the counters and the stove as she worked on their meal.

"I was thinking about what Armond said about amplifying my powers," Hayden told her.

"Do you know how you would be able to do that?" she asked.

"I have a theory," he said. "But we can test it out after dinner."

The two switched topics and discussed their plans for

the upcoming school year while Abby finished cooking dinner. After they finished eating, they moved to the living room couch.

"So, what's your idea?" Abby asked him.

"That shard…" Hayden started and then paused briefly to consider his words before continuing. "It does increase my power somewhat, but when I was trapped in the dreamscape with the orb and laid my hands on it, I felt a surge in power that was way beyond what the shard normally gives me."

"How does that help you now, though?" Abby questioned. "Didn't you destroy that orb?"

"I did destroy it," Hayden replied. "But I destroyed it inside the dreamscape. The orb was only a representation of the shard. The only reason that I was able to draw any power and knowledge from it was because it was the essence of the Alva'ci within the shard that pulled me into the dreamscape and not the other way around."

"So you think the shard holds all that same power?" Abby asked, now catching on to what Hayden was hinting at.

"Exactly!" Hayden declared. "But I've never been able to access that same amount of power from the shard for some reason."

"Maybe it's not as pure of a state as the orb was," Abby

offered.

"Yeah, you're probably on the right track," Hayden agreed. "We just have to find a way to change the shard into a purer form."

Hayden grabbed the shard from the coffee table and clenched it in his closed fist, focusing on drawing the most power from it that he could. The shard glowed so intensely that Abby could see it through Hayden's hand.

"If I had to put a number on it," Hayden told her as he released the shard. "That's only about fifteen percent of the power I felt contained in that orb."

Abby pondered the problem in her head for a few minutes and then hurriedly stood up, grabbing Hayden by the hand and leading him to the computer.

"Maybe the material is most pure in certain forms," Abby said excitedly. "The shard is a weird, jagged shape that obviously produces a lot less power than the shape of the orb."

"Okay…" Hayden said, asking Abby to continue.

"I can use the results of the analysis that Armond did on the material of the shard," she continued. "I'll feed that into an algorithm that tests for the most optimal power emission based on shape. I'll bet you that an orb-like structure hits really high on the charts compared to a jagged shard."

"Then all we have to do is change the shape of the

shard to match your results to get maximum power?" Hayden postulated.

"That's my theory," she agreed. "But with how hard this material is, it's going to be completely up to you to somehow change the shape of it."

"I can do that," Hayden said confidently as he recalled destroying the Alva'ci's armor that was made of the same material.

Abby furiously entered keystrokes on Hayden's computer and fed in the shard's material makeup data. She read the results to Hayden as they processed.

"Jagged shard, thirteen percent," she began. "Square, seven percent... diamond, thirty-five percent... hexagon, twenty-seven percent... octagon, ten percent... marquise, seventy percent... round, or orb-like, ninety-four percent!"

"You were right," Hayden told her.

"Wait a sec..." Abby interrupted him. "Pear or teardrop cut, ninety-nine percent."

"Wow," Hayden said in shock. "That's virtually completely pure."

Abby was giddy with excitement from the results. "Do you think you can change it to that?" she asked.

"Let's find out," Hayden stated. "We're going to need a place where there won't be a lot of eyes on us."

The duo decided to travel to the El Mirage dry lakebed in the high desert area of Southern California.

"Do you want me to drive?" Abby offered, knowing Hayden might be exhausted.

"Let's not drive," Hayden countered.

Abby looked at him, slightly confused. Hayden led her outside and told her to hold on to him. Abby only then realized what he had meant by not driving.

"Flying?" she asked nervously.

"Yeah," Hayden replied. "Don't worry, you'll be fine as long as you hold on."

Abby cautiously approached Hayden and put her arms around him, gripping him tightly. Hayden slowly rose a foot off the ground to acclimate Abby to the experience. Once she eased up and agreed she was okay, Hayden ascended higher into the sky.

"Are you still okay?" he asked her.

"I think so," she replied. "We're already up here, so no turning back now."

Hayden set course for El Mirage and sped through the sky. The duo landed on the lakebed three minutes later.

"Much faster than driving, right?" Hayden joked.

Abby looked like she was cherishing having her feet back on the ground. Hayden led the way to an area on the lakebed clear of any debris.

"Let's give this a try," Hayden told Abby as he set the shard down on a large flat stone. "Stay about twenty feet back from it."

Abby watched as Hayden recited the words to some spells. She had never seen him do this in person before.

"Emiratus, Amal Esta Preavius," Hayden spoke. "Chantiatus."

Forcefields surrounded Abby and Hayden. He then pointed one hand toward the shard and used the power of energy manipulation to draw power from it. With the other hand, he released a massive mixture of the other powers combined into a singular energy blast into the energy portal he had summoned.

Abby watched on in amazement as an unbelievably large column of energy flowed down from the night sky and hit the shard. It continued to flow for minutes as Hayden used the energy manipulation power to twist at the shard.

"Is it working?" she yelled out to Hayden.

He only responded by smiling back at her. Hayden continued to twist his hand, a look of severe determination across his face and sweat dripping from his brow. After another ten minutes of relentless work, Hayden clenched both of his fists closed. The energy blast disappeared.

Abby looked around and noticed that stirred-up dust from the lakebed was blanketing the air for miles. Through the haze, she could see an almost blinding light shining from where the shard had been placed. Hayden approached it and picked it up, the glow now fading as it rested in his hand. He walked over to Abby and showed her the results.

"It's perfect," she said with a sense of wonder evident in her tone. "You did it!"

"We did it, Abby," he corrected and gave her a hug.

"Does it work?" Abby asked him.

"Let's test it out," Hayden told her.

Hayden tightened his fist around the stone, and it began to glow fiercely. Swirls of orange aura surrounded Hayden's body.

"I can feel the enhanced power," he told Abby. "It's even greater than what I felt with the orb."

Hayden swung his other hand from side to side as if he were cutting through the air. A cylinder of fire and lightning fifty feet in diameter, spinning with the intensity of a tornado, rose from the ground into the sky. Beams of dark energy spewed from the firestorm, blacking out large swathes of the sky from their vision. The earth began to rumble beneath Hayden and Abby's feet as boulders and debris rose from the ground. Abby looked over at Hayden with an expression of awe-induced terror. Hayden opened his fist from the stone, and the landscape around them returned to normal.

"I'm sorry if I scared you," Hayden apologized.

"A little bit," she confessed. "I've just never seen anything like that before."

"Well, I'd say it worked," Hayden boasted.

"Yeah, definitely…" Abby mumbled.

"Let's head back?" Hayden asked her.

Abby didn't say a word in response, but she walked up to Hayden and put her arms around him. The duo vanished into the night sky and landed back in Fullerton minutes later. They headed back inside Hayden's apartment, and he led her out to the back patio.

"I have an idea," he told her. "To make this thing easier to carry around."

Abby watched as Hayden gathered random pieces of metal and leather from various bins. He placed the stone on the ground next to the items he had grabbed and activated his powers. Abby looked on as the metals melded in a simple outline around the edges of the stone, and the leather wrapped around itself to form a strong band of material. Hayden picked the finished pieces up from the ground and fed the leather band through a loop at the top of the metal. He tied the leather to form a necklace and placed the completed product around his neck.

"An amulet," Hayden said with a brim of accomplishment.

"It looks good," Abby told him. "Dan and Armond are going to be surprised when they come back and see this!"

"Yeah, seriously!" Hayden agreed.

Abby and Hayden walked back inside the apartment and plopped down on the couch, exhausted from the night's events.

"Do you mind if I stay here tonight?" Abby asked him.

"No, not at all," he responded. "I can set up the pull-out couch bed for you."

"Thank you," she replied with a sigh. "I'm so tired I don't think I could drive back home."

Hayden walked to the kitchen and tossed Abby a bottle of water from across the room. As he walked back into the front room, he noticed for the first time how dirty they were.

"That lakebed dust really did a number on us," he joked.

Abby looked down at her clothing and her arms and saw what Hayden was talking about. She was covered in dirt.

"How about this…" Hayden recommended. "I'll grab you some of my pajama pants and a shirt. You can jump in the guest shower to wash off, just toss your clothes out in the hallway before you get in, and I'll put them in the washing machine on a quick cycle. By the time you get out, they'll be in the dryer and ready for you to wear in the morning."

"Thank you, Hayden," she replied. "That's really considerate of you."

"No problem," he assured her and walked down to his bedroom. He returned a minute later with a pair of fleece pajama pants and one of the softer t-shirts that he could find in his closet. He held them up in the air momentarily to show them to Abby.

"I'll put these on the counter in the bathroom for you," Hayden told her. "I'm going to stay out here, just like knock on the bathroom door when you've put your clothes in the hallway, and I'll get them in the washer."

"Will do," she replied, following Hayden to the guest bathroom. He placed the pajamas on the counter and returned to the front room, eating a couple of snack-size chocolate candies from the dish on the coffee table while he waited.

Abby looked herself up and down in the mirror and realized that she had underestimated how much dust she was covered in. She walked over and turned on the shower to let it warm up. Abby returned to her place in front of the mirror and removed her shirt and pants as slowly and carefully as she could to avoid shaking dust loose onto the bathroom floor.

She wondered if one cycle through the washing machine would even be enough to get all the dust out of her clothes. Abby continued to undress, removing her bra and panties and placing them on top of her pants and shirt.

"Okay, time to soothe my tired body in that hot water," she thought to herself, looking forward to a nice shower.

Abby opened the bathroom door and peeked her head out, trying to keep her nude body inside the bathroom. She could hear Hayden out in the living room watching videos on his TikTok feed. She grabbed her clothes from the counter and placed them in the hallway next to the bathroom door. Instead of knocking as Hayden had suggested, she just called out to him before she slipped back into the bathroom.

"Clothes are in the hallway!" she said in a raised voice.

"Alright!" Hayden responded to her.

Abby closed the door and stepped into the shower, enjoying the heat and trickling water down her body as the dirt washed away.

Hayden grabbed Abby's neat pile of clothes from the hallway and walked back to the front room. Similarly to Abby's observation in the bathroom, he wondered if the washing machine would work with just one quick cycle. Hayden decided to do a little makeshift pre-cleaning. Since their pants and shirts were the articles of clothing that were mainly permeated with dirt, Hayden left Abby's bra and panties on the coffee table and took the other items out to the back patio with him.

Hayden held Abby's pants and shirt out in front of him and used his other hand to activate the power of Air. A steady wind whipped all around Hayden. A large portion of the dust from his and Abby's clothes drifted away on the current of air. Delighted with the success of his ingenious idea, Hayden walked back inside, grabbed Abby's undergarments from the coffee table, and made his way to the laundry room. He placed her clothes into the washer, added soap, and started the machine up. Hayden sat at the kitchen table, snacking on more miniature candy bars as he waited fifteen minutes for the washing machine to finish.

Hayden tossed the candy wrappers in the trash as he headed back to the laundry room. He took Abby's bra and hung it on a hanger by the laundry room door. He tossed her remaining clothes in the dryer with a fabric softener sheet and started it up.

Hayden walked down the hallway to his bedroom, noting that the shower was still on in the guest bathroom. He entered his bathroom and tossed his dirty clothes in the laundry basket to be washed later. He then enjoyed a nice hot shower.

___

Twenty minutes later, Hayden returned to the front room to find Abby watching television on the couch in her pajamas. Hayden pulled out the couch bed for her and asked if she needed anything. After they said their goodnights, Hayden rolled into his bed and immediately fell asleep.

وقت

Chapter Eleven

Leaps and Bounds

Dan and Armond arrived back at Hayden's apartment at 9:00 a.m., eager to try and make progress with finding Kali.

"Abby is already here?" Dan mused, noticing her car in the driveway.

Hayden answered the door and walked with Dan and Armond to the living room, where Abby was already sitting.

"Hey…" Dan said with suspicion in his voice. "Those are the same clothes you wore yesterday, aren't they, Abby?"

"Yes, Dan, they are…" she replied. "I stayed the night here. Hayden and I worked on something important after you guys left."

"Working on something?" Dan repeated, raising an eyebrow at her.

"Asshole, not that!" she quipped back at him, dispelling the sexual innuendo he was insinuating.

"For real," Hayden chimed in. "We were working on how to amplify my powers. Abby came up with an idea, and we figured out that if we reshaped the shard, the power I can draw from it increases tremendously."

"Wait, what?" Armond now joined the conversation.

Hayden pulled the amulet out from underneath his shirt and held it so Dan and Armond could see it.

"You should see what he can do with that thing," Abby excitedly told them as they gazed at the amulet.

"What can you do with that?" Armond asked cautiously.

"We tapped into almost a hundred percent purity in the stone's power," Hayden told him. "It's unprecedented."

"Take my word for it," Abby told them. "Last night he created a tornado of fire and lightning that was at least fifty feet in diameter, and it was the most amazing and the scariest thing that I've ever seen."

"Can you use it to enhance your search for Kali, though?" Armond asked, switching the focus away from the effects on Hayden's other powers.

"We haven't tried yet," Hayden admitted. "By the time we got back, we were exhausted, so we just went to bed."

"Well, let's try now," Armond insisted.

Hayden grabbed the list from the coffee table and read off the name of one of the planets he had failed to see the day before.

"Alright, here we go," he said confidently.

Hayden grasped the amulet in his hand, and it shined with a dazzling orange light. He closed his eyes and waited for a few minutes. Finally, the planet came into his vision. Hayden searched above and below the surface for any signs of life or movement.

"Nothing on that planet," Hayden said as he opened his eyes.

"It worked?" Dan asked. "That was a whole lot shorter than the ones you did yesterday."

"Yeah, it worked," Hayden told him with a smile on his face.

"Okay, let's get through some of these and find Kali," Armond said, finally showing some semblance of happiness.

Hayden spent the next hour scanning through five more of the planets on the list without finding any signs of Kali or the Alva'ci.

"I need to stop," Hayden admitted. "The further the planets get away from us, the more draining it is to visualize them and maintain that connection. I feel like I just ran an entire marathon in an hour."

"You need to be careful," Armond told Hayden. "I think that the power inside that amulet may be more than you bargained for."

"I will hone my skills with it," Hayden replied. "This amulet has incredible potential."

"Okay, I trust you, Hayden," Armond said. "I am going to head home. I have a video call with Shaun and Lora in thirty minutes to check in on them."

Hayden nodded, and Armond departed. Abby excused herself to use the restroom while Dan and Hayden went out to the back patio to enjoy some fresh air.

"Dude," Dan said to Hayden. "You've got to show me those new powers."

"They're not new powers," Hayden said while laughing. "They're just more… potent. Maybe after I relax for a bit, we can all go out tonight, and I'll show you."

Abby walked out onto the back patio and joined Hayden and Dan.

"You down for an adventure tonight?" Dan asked Abby. "Hayden said he would show off those enhanced powers."

Abby laughed at Dan's question. "I'm down for it, but if we're going to be out that late again, I should probably go get a change of clothes just in case."

The trio spent the remainder of the day relaxing. As night fell, Hayden ordered takeout for them to share. After dinner, Hayden asked Dan and Abby if they were ready to go.

To stay within driving distance, Hayden suggested that they go to a sparsely frequented section of beach between Newport and Huntington. Once they arrived, Hayden didn't waste any time showing Dan his enhanced powers since he was still quite exhausted from the day.

Hayden grasped the amulet in his hand, and as it started to glow, he flew out just over the surface of the ocean. After about a half mile, he turned around and headed back towards his friends on the shore. As he flew towards them, blindingly bright light, crackling with electricity, emanated from his sides. Just before he reached the shore, Hayden sent a beam of fire straight up into the sky. As Hayden touched down on the beach, Dan and Abby ran up to him.

"That was impressive," Dan admitted. "I feel sorry for anyone or anything that ends up fighting you in the future."

Hayden laughed out loud at Dan's remark. All decidedly tired, the group agreed to head back to Fullerton. When they arrived back at Hayden's apartment, Dan and Abby jumped in their respective cars and headed out for the night. Hayden fell asleep right after his head hit the pillow for the second night in a row.

The group met at Hayden's apartment for the next three days. Hayden ran through five planets from the list each day to look for Kali. The fourth day was seemingly shaping up to be just like the others.

"Wait," Hayden paused, his eyes still closed. "There's something there on the far side of that planet."

"Really?!" Abby exclaimed.

Hayden concentrated on visualizing what he had found. There were definite heat signatures and signs of life as he honed his focus on the area.

"I found them!" Hayden yelled as he opened his eyes to the group. "I felt Kali out there."

Hayden grabbed the pen from the coffee table and circled the entry on the list for the planet. His hand was shaking in nervous excitement.

"What do we do now?" Dan asked.

"That is the next part of the rescue that we need a plan for," Armond said. "This planet is very far away from Earth. We cannot travel there with any kind of spacecraft."

"So, then what?" Dan asked, confused that now all of a sudden, the rescue mission seemed impossible.

"I'm not sure," Armond admitted. "Even with the

amulet, Hayden cannot fly fast enough to reach those distances in his lifetime… and that's assuming he would even survive. He would have no extra food or water with him."

"So this is impossible?" Dan asked, now vocalizing his thoughts.

"Perhaps we can draw the Alva'ci back here to Earth?" Armond spoke the first idea that came to mind.

"Wouldn't that be like really dangerous?" Abby asked.

"You're right," Armond conceded. "I'm just speaking from the top of my head. The Alva'ci wreaked havoc the last time it was here."

"I've been thinking about this," Hayden interjected. "The Alva'ci was able to open a portal and, I assume, travel directly to the planet where it has Kali. If the amulet holds the same power as the Alva'ci has, I should be able to learn how to open those same portals."

"Whoa," Dan said. "That's a good idea."

"That may not be a good idea," Armond advised him. "We have no way of knowing how those portals work or if Hayden would be able to control them."

"As far as I see it, it's the only real option we have right now," Hayden stated.

"Can you do that?" Abby asked Hayden.

"No, not yet, at least," he told her. "But I can try."

"I'll help you any way that I can," she replied.

"Yeah, me too," Dan said in agreement.

The group looked over to Armond. "If you can open a portal and you feel confident enough to actually use one, then I suppose you're correct that it's our only shot."

The group adjourned the official meeting for the day, and Armond left for home to meet his brother, who was coming to visit from New York. Dan and Abby stayed behind and continued to encourage Hayden to attempt to learn how to open a portal.

"I'm thinking that there's only one place I'll be able to learn how to do this," Hayden told them. "Do you guys want to see what the dreamscape is like?"

"Yes," both Abby and Dan answered in unison.

"Okay, get ready," Hayden said as he sat in between them on the couch. "Make sure you're leaning back into the couch so you don't fall over forward when you knock out."

Abby and Dan did as he instructed. Hayden placed a hand on each of their shoulders and took them into the dreamscape with him.

Hayden, Abby, and Dan appeared in the middle of a clearing surrounded by dense forest. Abby spun around and admired the vast beauty of the land around them. Dan stared in amazement at the rich detail in every possible aspect of the trees, rocks, and clouds.

"What are you wearing, Abby?" Dan asked her jokingly.

Abby looked down at her outfit. She had on a short white dress embellished with a lace floral pattern.

"What do you mean, Dan?" she replied. "It's a cute dress."

Dan looked down and examined his clothes to find he was wearing black slacks and a short-sleeved button-down shirt.

"Hayden, why the formal attire?" Dan joked again.

"I didn't put painstaking thought into what we were all going to be wearing," Hayden replied. "I'm a little preoccupied with the goal, so be glad you're not naked."

"You can do that?" Abby asked with a nervous laugh.

"If I felt so inclined to, yes, I could do that," Hayden replied with a smirk.

Abby laughed and continued to look around at the scenery. Hayden positioned himself in the middle of the clearing and held on to the amulet, concentrating on the goal of deepening his powers and finding new ones. After several minutes, Hayden opened his eyes and extended his hand in front of him. He focused on trying to create a portal. Dan and Abby now watched in anticipation.

For a moment, a flicker of swirling orange appeared in front of Hayden… a small opening, far too minuscule for a human to enter. Just as quickly as it appeared, it vanished. Hayden tried again several times with the same results.

"You made one!" Abby said happily.

"Yeah, but there's no way I could use that," Hayden replied. "Even if it weren't way too small, it's unstable."

"You're just going to have to keep practicing then, right?" Dan asked.

Hayden shook his head to agree. He told Abby and Dan that the exercise had worn him out, and he drew the group out of the dreamscape. They woke back up on the couch and agreed that they were all famished. They spent the next few hours at Eduardo Quesada's Mexican Restaurant, having dinner and drinks.

ℭℨ ℭℨ ℭℨ ℭℨ ℭℨ ℭℨ

TWENTY WEEKS LATER

December 19

Hayden had spent the previous months developing his abilities to create portals, both inside and outside of the dreamscape. The fall semester had begun, so he spent as much spare time as possible working with the amulet in between classes, clubs, and hanging out with friends.

Hayden woke up at 5:00 a.m. so that he would have some extra time before his Monday morning class began. He had felt that he was on the edge of a breakthrough in his efforts to finally keep a stable portal open. It had been three weeks since he had accomplished his goal of creating one that was large enough to accommodate a person his size.

He began the morning by grabbing the amulet from his nightstand and heading to the living room. Hayden walked through the steps that he had become all too familiar with and opened a bright orange portal in the room before him. He focused on keeping the object open, and to his surprise, the field seemed stable.

He cautiously approached the portal in the middle of his living room and looked back at the clock hanging on the wall. "Only 5:30, plenty of time left to get ready," he thought to himself. Hayden stepped towards the edge of the portal, slightly nervous about the unknown effect that it would have. He attempted to walk through the field and was surprised by what he saw. A vast expanse of dark space was stretched out before him, a planet fixed in the distance.

Just as the wonder of what he was seeing began to process in his mind, he was pushed backward out of the portal and into his living room. The portal closed in front of him as Hayden stood there, still dumbfounded by what he had seen. He walked to the bathroom and started running the shower so that he could get ready for his class as he ran the possibilities through his mind.

Upon arriving at campus, Hayden caught up with Dan and Abby before heading to class. He wanted to update them on what he had done this morning.

"So, I finally had one stable for long enough to step inside," Hayden proclaimed to his friends.

"Wait, you actually went inside it?" Abby questioned.

"I tried to," he corrected his previous statement. "I was kind of in, and I could see space and a planet on the other side. Then a few seconds later, it felt like I was pushed back out and back in my living room."

"Maybe you just need a running start," Dan said jokingly.

"Actually, you might be right," Hayden said as he contemplated what Dan had said.

"You should try it again when we're all done with classes for the day," Abby insisted. "This time with us there, though."

"Sounds like a plan," Hayden agreed. "Let's grab some lunch after class and then head back to my place."

———

The trio agreed on the plan and then headed off on their separate ways to get to their classes. Hayden tried his hardest to pay attention during his developmental biology class instead of letting himself drift off in thought about how close he was to finally being able to rescue Kali.

After Hayden's second and final class of the day, he met up with Abby and Dan in the student union building to grab a quick lunch. The meal was unusually quiet and rushed as all three of the friends focused on returning to Hayden's apartment. Thirty minutes later, when they finally arrived, Dan and Abby tossed their bags next to the couch and eagerly waited for Hayden to show them what he had done.

"We ready?" Hayden asked them.

"More than ready, bro," Dan replied, vocalizing the anticipation in the room.

"Alright, first, I think I'm going to try something easier," Hayden told them. "I'll make a portal to my bedroom. It's not very far away, so maybe just walking through the field will be possible. Then we can work our way up in distance and see what happens."

Abby and Dan nodded their heads in agreement with the plan. Hayden stepped back from the couch to the middle of the living room and clutched the amulet. A few seconds later, a portal appeared five feet in front of him.

Hayden walked toward the portal. The tension and anticipation in the room was almost palpable. As Hayden stepped into the portal, Abby gasped at the prospect of what was actually happening in front of her.

The portal disappeared after Hayden entered. Dan and Abby exchanged eyes-wide-open glances and then sprung from the couch and ran down the hallway to Hayden's bedroom as if they shared the same thought. As they entered the room, they saw the orange flash of the portal disappearing as Hayden stepped out of it. Abby, overcome with excitement, fell to her knees as she processed the seemingly impossible.

"It worked," Hayden stated the obvious.

"It's incredible," Abby added.

After taking a few minutes to recover from the realization of what had just been achieved, the trio returned to the living room, and Hayden began to further test his ability with destinations located further away. He was able to easily teleport himself to his front yard, the end of the neighborhood, and to the local library.

"Let's try and up the challenge now," he suggested.

"Where to now?" Dan asked.

"How about Arizona?" Hayden said. "That's a few hundred miles."

Hayden opened another portal in front of him. This

time he increased his pace to a jog as he entered the field. The portal in the living room closed. Dan and Abby waited patiently in suspense.

The sand on the beach of Lake Havasu indented as Hayden's feet slid through it on the other side of the portal. A group of children swimming in the nearby water stopped, frozen in awe as they witnessed the spectacle. Hayden waved at them before ascending into the sky and flying back to Fullerton. Hayden opened the front door of his apartment to see Abby and Dan still sitting on the couch, waiting for his return.

"Did it work?!" Dan asked in a rapid cadence.

"Sure did," Hayden answered. "I just flew back from Havasu."

"You were only gone for like three minutes," Abby said, astounded.

"Let's keep on going," Hayden told them excitedly.

Hayden proceeded to take portals to various states and eventually made a jump all the way to Italy. At the conclusion of the last jump, the group deliberated on where to have dinner and, in a force of habit, decided to head to their favorite Mexican restaurant in town.

"Hey, just a thought," Hayden mused aloud to Dan and Abby. "What if we all took a portal to the restaurant?"

"Is that possible?" Abby asked him.

"There's only one way to find out," Hayden suggested mischievously.

Abby and Dan looked at each other for a few moments as if they were debating the idea without speaking.

"Let's do it," Dan told him.

Hayden smirked and opened a portal in front of the group. He interlocked his arms with Abby and Dan, then led them in a running start through the field.

"Holy shit!" Dan exclaimed as they appeared in the restaurant's parking lot, the portal disappearing behind them in a flash of orange.

"I can't believe I just did that," Abby admitted.

After Abby and Dan took a moment to recover from their first experience with instantaneous travel, the group of friends entered the restaurant and celebrated the day with their fill of drinks and dinner.

ᏝᎧ ᏝᎧ ᏝᎧ ᏝᎧ ᏝᎧ ᏝᎧ

The next morning, Hayden called Armond and told him about all his developments with creating portals the day before.

"You actually used one?" Armond asked him.

"I used about a dozen of them," Hayden told Armond proudly.

"Where did you go?" Armond asked.

"Local places at first," Hayden informed him. "Then I kept going further away. I even went to another country."

"That's amazing," Armond admitted. "Do you think you can go further than that?"

"I'm going to try today," Hayden told him. "Dan and Abby are coming over at 2:00 p.m. after we get out of classes for the day if you want to join us."

"I'll meet you there," Armond told him and then ended the call.

Hayden's classes for the day flew by. He arrived at his apartment to see Dan, Abby, and Armond already waiting for him outside. The group filed into the living room and sat in anticipation as Hayden readied himself.

"So, you're trying for the moon?" Armond asked.

"Yep, that's the plan," Hayden replied.

"I would advise you to cast a Chantiatus spell on yourself before you go through," Armond told Hayden. "I have no idea if it will help you breathe once you get to the other side, but let's hope so. Either way, I would be quick with coming back."

"Good idea," Hayden said and chanted the spell. A

forcefield immediately surrounded him.

Hayden opened the portal in front of him and took a running start through it. Thirty seconds later, another portal opened in the living room, and Hayden came back through it.

"So?" Dan asked him.

"Call me Neil Armstrong 'cause your boy has been to the moon," Hayden joked as he laughed joyfully.

Abby sat in stunned silence as Armond got up and paced around the room in thought.

"You could breathe?" he asked Hayden.

"Yeah, the forcefield worked just like you hoped," Hayden replied.

"Are you going to try for the planet that Kali is at?" Armond asked, the tone of his voice changing from triumphant to serious.

Hayden took a deep breath, and his demeanor changed to match Armond's voice. "Let's do it," he said.

"Hayden, don't you think you should prepare yourself first," Abby asked him, her voice giving away the fact that she was worried for him.

"I just want to see if I can make the jump," he reassured Abby. "I'll come right back. No rescue yet, no fighting."

"Okay," she gave Hayden her approval.

The group watched on nervously as Hayden opened

another portal. He dashed toward it and disappeared into the field. The group watched as the portal remained in the room, unlike all of the previous ones. Moments later, Hayden stumbled back through the field and landed on his back.

"That's what happened before," Hayden said as he picked himself up from the carpet. "I must not be going through the portal fast enough, even with running."

"How about flying into it?" Abby suggested.

"Genius idea," he replied, smiling at Abby.

"If the speed needed is related to the distance, maybe we should make some calculations first," Armond suggested.

The group huddled together around Abby's laptop and crunched the numbers.

"How fast can you fly?" Abby asked Hayden.

"With the amulet and a forcefield up," Hayden answered. "The fastest I've been able to get to is 1,412 miles per hour."

"Wow," Dan muttered in shock.

"You're 110 miles per hour too slow by my calculations," Abby told Hayden. "For the distance this planet is, you'll have to get to Mach Two… 1,522 miles per hour."

Hayden thought momentarily and did some math in his head as he paced around the living room.

"Okay, I've got it," he told the group.

Hayden opened a portal and ran through. Abby, Dan, and Armond waited on the couch nervously, awaiting his return. Their discomfort was increased by the fact that Hayden hadn't even told them his plan.

A flash of orange appeared on the observation deck of a popular skyscraper in Midtown Manhattan. Hayden stepped out of the portal amidst crowds of tourists who began to take pictures and approach him after seeing him appear from nowhere. Hayden gave the onlookers a brief friendly wave and walked to the edge of the observation deck.

Several tourists gasped, and others covered their children's eyes as Hayden climbed over the thick glass partitions at the edge of the deck. He released a deep nervous breath as he stood at the edge of the building's stonework. A throng of onlookers formed against the glass partition behind him, taking pictures and video.

"Chantiatus," Hayden said under his breath, a force-field forming around him, prompting a commotion of voices from the onlookers.

Hayden grasped the amulet in his hand and looked at the street below him. An intense orange light emanated from the amulet as Hayden leapt head first off the building. The crowd of onlookers erupted in panicked screams, and the resultant videos on the internet were trending within minutes.

Immediately after jumping from the building, Hayden accelerated at full speed in flight toward the ground. As he neared street level, Hayden opened a portal just above the sidewalk and flew straight into it.

Back in Fullerton, Dan and Abby's phones began to chime incessantly with notifications. Dan pulled out his phone and, after inspecting the screen for a moment, held it up so that Abby and Armond could see it. He opened the notification and began to play the video.

As they were watching the scene from New York on Dan's phone, Hayden reappeared in the living room. He walked through the portal to see his friend's mouths agape in disbelief. He shook his head at the group to indicate that the plan had, indeed, worked.

"Quite the scene you caused testing that theory," Abby told him, still reeling from the footage in the multitude of online videos that had popped up within minutes.

Hayden shrugged and threw his hands up.

"Who doesn't like a little bit of theatrics once in a while?"

Epilogue

Hayden looked out across the expanse of the cemetery as he sat next to Paige's headstone. After all of the madness, the loss, the heartbreak, and the breakthroughs of the last few months, Hayden felt an overwhelming sense of guilt that he hadn't come here more often. He brushed his palm over the blades of grass as he spoke to his friend.

"Paige, I really wish that you were here. Life hasn't been the same without you. Graduation is coming next year, and I always imagined that would be a moment of accomplishment we would share together. But also, I'm glad you aren't here to suffer through your sister being taken. I know how painful and stressful this situation would be for you because I know how it is for me. I promise I will get to her and bring her back."

The long sigh of contemplation Hayden released seemed to echo in the almost eerie silence around him. He asked himself why he was talking to a gravestone when he could just speak to Paige. Hayden touched his fingers to his forehead and transported himself into the dreamscape. The scene he awoke to inside was the same as the outside world. The dreamscape version of the cemetery was the same in every way, with the lone exception of Paige sitting atop a nearby stone bench. She was dressed in her favorite hoodie sweatshirt and a pair of jeans. He walked over and sat beside her, taking her hand in his.

"I miss you, Paige. Everyone misses you. You know how they all are. Dan is like the spring sun… warm and friendly, always trying to make each of us feel better in any situation. Sometimes shining a light on areas that are still covered in frost, perhaps thawing them out before people are ready. Clark and Samantha are lately like the moon, here and then gone again. Ever since they started dating each other, their presence wanes and waxes, always welcome but always changing. Abby is like the ocean. Though some may disagree with that sentiment or that comparison, I know Abby all too well. Like the ocean, she can be a place of peace and quiet strength. A calm and tranquil thing of majestic beauty, yet hiding a fearsome power underneath the surface. But you were always Sirius, the brightest star in the night sky. Even when the moon was gone, you always lit up all of our lives. You radiated that light and positivity with a steady and unrelenting glow. You made every one of us want to achieve more so that we could shine like you. Lately, I feel like the darkness. I felt the searingly intense power that resides in me and the corruption that lives on the edge of that power. Honestly, if you hadn't been a part of my life, I feel like I might have gone over that edge. That darkness is like a stormcloud perched on the horizon, always waiting."

"Your light is coming, Hayden," Paige told him as she stood up from the bench. "The light shall mingle with the darkness, and together they shall shine with a brilliance both dazzling and fearsome."

Hayden tried to speak to ask her what she meant, but Paige placed her finger over Hayden's lips to silence him. Hayden stared in wonder at his friend. She smiled at Hayden and placed her fingers on his forehead… Hayden was thrown out of the dreamscape and back into reality. He stumbled back up to his feet and looked at Paige's headstone in a state of disbelief.

Glancing down at his watch, Hayden discovered that he was now almost running late for Dan's New Year's Eve party. He shook his head and chuckled as he contemplated how bizarre his life was sometimes.

"I'll come to see you again soon, Paige," Hayden said, now speaking to the gravestone again. "Tonight, I'll raise a toast in your honor, and every one of us will drink to your memory."

Before he left, Hayden picked up a rock from the ground near Paige's grave and gripped it tightly in his hand. The symbol of the power Light illuminated on the back of his hand. He placed the transformed rock on top of Paige's headstone. It shone like a miniature star, illuminating several dozen feet around her plot for hours after Hayden departed.

"A star, just like you," he said as he turned and walked back toward his car.

෨ ෨ ෨ ෨ ෨ ෨

Hayden made good time over to Dan's apartment and arrived only ten minutes after everyone else. Dan immediately approached him with a couple of beers fresh from the refrigerator. He popped the lids off and handed one to Hayden.

"Time to catch up, buddy!" Dan yelled at him over the music. "Clark and I are ahead of you by three already."

Hayden laughed at his friend's eagerness to get the

party started and took a swig of his beer. Dan walked off to greet two more latecomers as they walked through the front door. Hayden took a moment to look around the room. Clark and Samantha were in the dining room, in conversation with one another. Abby stood in the kitchen, sipping on a mixed drink and half-listening to a group of people that were gathered in the same semi-circle. The remainder of the apartment was filled with several dozen other people. Hayden was slightly surprised that they all shared that many acquaintances and extended friends. He watched as a group of people in the living room danced to "Mo Bamba" by Sheck Wes.

Abby walked from the kitchen and made her way over to Hayden, holding her drink up in the air and dancing to the song, prompting Hayden to join her. After the music and dance ended, Abby hugged Hayden and welcomed him to the party. Dan then rejoined both his friends after showing the party's newcomers where the drinks and snacks were.

"Bro, thanks for bringing over all your party stuff and setting it up yesterday," Dan told Hayden. "These lights make the party ten times better if you ask me!"

Hayden had brought over his large assortment of LED PAR-style lights and lasers that reacted to the music, along with a fog machine. The two friends had spent several hours the night before setting up the lights and testing them out for maximum visual stimulation.

"Yeah, everyone seems to like the vibe," Hayden replied.

As the hours wore on and midnight grew closer, the group of friends immersed themselves in the atmosphere of the party. Hayden let himself enjoy the night and reveled in the celebration. After several rounds of drinks and shots, the group congregated in the dining room amid dozens of people.

"A toast!" Dan exclaimed over the music and the conversations of other partygoers.

"What do you toast to?!" Clark yelled, egging his friend on.

"To all of us! To Hayden, Abby, Clark, Samantha… to all of you here tonight! May the new year treat us well!"

Abby decided to join in on the festivities. "A toast to Hayden! His friendship has meant the world to me and even changed my life. Not to mention that he literally saved every single person in this room!"

The crowd cheered, raised their glasses in a collective toast, and took a drink. Hayden smiled flippantly at Abby for reminding the group of his newfound fame but then placed his hand on her shoulder and smiled more sincerely at her for the meaning behind the toast.

"One more toast!" Hayden yelled. "This one to Paige.

Our dear friend, we wish you were here with us tonight to celebrate a new year. Your legacy lives on in everything that we do."

The room fell almost silent for a few moments as Hayden's somber toast hit everyone's ears. Just as instantly, the crowd erupted and bellowed in unison. "To Paige!" The party resumed as everyone drank a swig in her memory.

A few minutes later, Samantha called out to the group from the living room. "One minute, everyone!"

Groups of partygoers clamored about the apartment, gathering new drinks for the ritual midnight celebration and finding their closest friends and significant others to stand with as the clock ticked down.

Clark started the chant. "Ten, nine, eight…"

The entirety of the crowd joined in. As the clock struck midnight, the room roared with jubilation. Clark and Samantha shared a customary New Year's kiss before taking a drink. Hayden, Abby, and Dan looked at each other in quiet recognition that none of them had anyone to share the moment with like Clark and Samantha did.

Abby threw her hands in the air and communicated nonverbally that the three of them might as well serve each other's ephemeral ardor. "Oh, what the hell, right?"

Hayden laughed as he realized what she was proposing.

He shook his head in agreement. After all, the three of them had been through the impending end of the world together.

Yeah, what the hell, why not," Dan threw in his consent as well.

Hayden approached Abby, and she leaned in, grasping his face in her hands, as they shared a kiss. This drew the attention of Clark and Samantha, who started whooping and hollering at the scene. Hayden walked over to Dan, and the two friends held out their arms in jest before sharing a brief "bro-kiss." Now the larger group of people around them joined in the ruckus with Clark and Samantha. Finally, Abby walked over to Dan and shared a kiss with him to complete the trio's midnight spectacle.

As the commotion calmed down and the focus shifted back to the party, Hayden walked to the kitchen to retrieve a new round of drinks for Abby, Dan, and himself. Clark walked up beside him to get a fresh drink as well.

"You three are always the life of the party, eh!" Clark said to Hayden as he patted him on the shoulder.

Hayden handed Clark a new beer, and they clinked their bottles together in a mock toast.

"All five of us are the life of the party, my friend!" Hayden corrected him to include Samantha and Clark in the toast.

———

As he walked back toward the dining room to join the others, he listened to the song change on the stereo in the front room. Aptly timed, the piano notes and opening lines of Taylor Swift's song "New Year's Day" reverberated throughout the apartment. The lights that he and Dan had strategically placed throughout the space flooded the dimly lit party with a fluid accompaniment of soft blue and lavender hues. He smirked reminiscently as the song's chorus played. Something about those words had always sent a chill throughout his body, a mixture of hope, emotion, and longing. As he continued his journey to the dining room, Hayden felt a vibration his cell phone. He wondered who would be texting him as he pulled the phone out. All of his closest friends were here at the party with him, his parents had long since given up midnight celebrations in favor of extra sleep, and his siblings had texted earlier in the night since they were on vacation in Virginia. He tapped on the screen to open his messaging app and focused his vision on the message. He was mildly surprised at what he saw. The text was from Elle.

"I just smelled cinnamon, and it reminded me of your French toast. Random ik lol. Happy New Year, Hayden!"

"Happy New Year, Elle!" he texted back and then rejoined his friends to resume bidding adieu to a markedly life-changing year.

Appendix I

The Ancient Powers

The several powers, or magical abilities, are first seen in use in 54,000 BC. At that point in time, they became dormant in humans due to a spell performed by Abbas. Their traces were passed on, although they were undetectable to their bearers and the powers unusable.

In 2022, a prophecy came true when Hayden de Vere turned out to be the foretold cognizant one. The appearance of the cognizant one was prophesied by Abbas in a vision approximately two years after the Alva'ci came to Earth. As the bearers of the dormant powers began to die off in 2022, the powers began to manifest once again in their real forms.

Little information is known about the origination of the magical abilities and how or when humans acquired them. It is rumored that there is a book of lore, written by

Abbas when he was close to his death, that conveys the secrets that humans used to acquire their magical abilities. Whether or not this book exists is known only to the descendants of Abbas.

The Powers and Their Symbols:

Elemental Powers:

Water ماء   Fire نار

Earth أرض   Air جو

Sub-Elemental Powers:

Light ضوء   Energy طاقة

Shadow ظل   Electricity برق

Non-Elemental Powers:

Ane'illuminus / Thought خاطِر

The Seven Spells نوبات

The Seven Spells:

Abarus - Otherworldly Warriors

Tithethus - The Bindings

Emiratus - Power Amplification

Prophesch'naya Con'di Ashante - Shroud of Darkness

Chantiatus - Protective Forcefields

Youlvasius - Lucky Strikes

Amal Esta Preavius - Energy Portals

The Eighth Spell:

Nelitus Absoritum Malitus - Alva'ci Banishment

In 54,000 BC, Abbas used the combined magical abilities of his group to create an Eighth Spell. This spell was specifically for banishing the Alva'ci into a comatose state. This spell has only been used once in history. As a consequence of performing this spell, magical abilities disappeared from humans. The remnants of magical ability remained in a dormant state within ten people, who were thereafter known as the Agents of Fate. These dormant powers were passed down throughout the years, and their presence kept the Alva'ci from re-emerging.

Appendix II

The Prophecies

Among the collection of prophecies and visions recorded in the books of lore concerning the Agents of Fate, the following have been regarded as particularly prominent by the descendants of Abbas.

The Parisifian Prophecy
53998 BC

An eternal power subdued in flesh and bone.
Coming to light in a perilous world.
Among them stands a cognizant one,
with whom fate is vested…
causing life and love to be lost or won.

Destiny has issued us a lonely call.
In solitude, we find a universality.
We are the ones who lead the charge.
We shall hold the darkness at bay.
When among ten five shall fall,
the strength of their hand will be tested.
The trials of one led into darkness,
shall prove the end of an era.
These are the remnants of powers ancient,
these are the agents of fate.

The Abassilon Prophecy
53993 BC

At once, you awake and find yourself in a new world,
a new beginning.
The scars of time, though stinging at times,
are dulled from passing years.
Memories of nights that shall never be forgotten
flash through your mind from time to time,
to remind you of all that was had, of all that was lost.

You walk upon the sands,
on the beach of this new land..

———

journeying to something yet unknown.
You see a girl, standing alone by the water's edge.
Her golden hair flowing in the breeze, her voice fair and sweet.
Her eyes, while calm and inviting,
also piercing and hiding much behind them.

As you walk nearer, flashes of destiny
race through your mind like precognitive deja vu.
What path is coming to emerge?
You can feel it in your bones,
if you approach her, a piece of your life will be hers.

They've called you many things...
they focused on the darkness that swirled around you.
And though they were mistaken,
as magnificence can oft be mistook for darkness,
they never understood.
But as you look onward toward the girl,
you can see the light from within her.

...and the light shall mingle with the darkness, and together
they shall shine with a brilliance both dazzling and fearsome.

She turns to see you and you look into her eyes.

Suddenly you understand,
and together you walk toward the city.

~~E'it ad'a layadänte~~
We shall share this path

The Prophecy of Hindrant Salvas
53980 BC

Pacing the grounds, hollow footsteps echo into oblivion.
Turning round, facing the reality of duplicity.

Into the waters, knee-deep. The rip current drawing you in.
The seduction that you both play on each other
is providential.

What can you have?
Is it greater than anything you've been given?
What remains to be seen,
 shall determine the course of revisionist history.

Turning a corner into the halls of life yet written.
Through the doorway and into an empty room.

———

We have come to dance here,
a dance careful and indifferent.
Setting the night ablaze with aberrant passions.
The world outside these windows, vast and insignificant.
Who you are at dusk is not the you of dawn.

Reaching a precipice, fraught with lasting decisions.
How do you get what you want,
when what you want is everything?

Tirritus Elabus, a Vision
53952 BC

As I walk through these woods,
the freezing air seems to chill my very soul.
A cloud of darkness follows me,
covering the landscape behind me in impenetrable black.
I came to the water's edge, a lake, as still as glass.
Not a sound to be heard.
As I step into the water,
the ripples extend outward until the waters are again
as still as I.
Minutes pass, as I reflect on what has brought me here.

With a flick of the wrist,
the still silence is split with a flash of lightning,
tearing through the sky, blinding and beautiful.
The elements stand at my call.
The surrounding darkness evaporates
in the stroke of a heartbeat.
Time slows to a standstill, as the stars begin to shine…
Their reflection now paints the lake like a canvas.
The chill in my body, replaced with a fire,
burning through my veins.
I had come to this place to remind myself,
I held this power the entire time.

As you join me at the lake's edge,
with your own journey through tribulations…
I say to you, "Stand here next to me, take my hand
and I will teach you the way to conquer the darkness.
You are as I am, greater than the crowds that surround us.
I will show you how to transcend the past
and dictate the future.
Give your darkness to me, darling,
I will hold it to the light and transform it to tempered resolve.
More than respite, even to push back the chill within.
I will paint you with fire,

———

and I will dress you with magnificence…
and all the world will see your brilliance."

But for this moment, while time still stands frozen,
take my hand and feel the warmth emanating.
A tiny spark of a fire raging inside.
Gaze into the night sky with me
and know what it is to feel infinite,
and trust that I will never let you fall.

AGENTS OF FATE

Appendix III

The Books of Lore

Abbas wrote several books that were passed down to the firstborn of each generation of his family. These books contained the lore concerning the Agents of Fate. The current keeper of the books of lore is Armond el-Hashem. Among the known volumes are:

The Conqueror الفاتح

An account of the arrival of the Alva'ci on Earth. This book contains first-hand accounts from Abbas, Ahjiamed, Koshili, and dozens of other members of their village. Also included are charts and drawings depicting the creature, a sky chart detailing where the Alva'ci entered the atmosphere, and a description of the orange rock that the creature's armor consisted of.

Prophecies and Visions نبوءات ورؤى

After the victory obtained over the Alva'ci in 54,000 BC, Abbas began to have visions pertaining to the nature of the Agents of Fate and future events that concerned those that held the remnants of power. This book of lore is a collection of the visions and prophecies that Abbas made until his death at the age of 387. One of the most prominent prophecies included was The Parisifian Prophecy. This prophecy foretold the eventual appearance of the Cognizant One, an Agent of Fate that was unique in their abilities and would come at a time in history when the Alva'ci may possess the ability to rise again.

Powers and Practices القدرات والمهارات
(aka Abilities and Skills)

Written very late in the life of Abbas, this book of lore's existence is only rumored. It is said that this book includes detailed explanations of how humans first acquired magical abilities. Details of each magical power and its uses are included, ranging from the simplest forms to advanced techniques that came with aptitude and skill. The book includes a detailed account of the power of Ane'illuminus and the achievements made by those that mastered the power within their lifetimes. A section of the lore includes an account of how Abbas and a handful of others were able to artificially extend their lives to seemingly unnatural ages through the masterful use of the magical powers. Finally, Abbas included warnings concerning the use of The Forbidden Spell (which is mentioned in The Abassilon Prophecy, but with the words crossed out to prevent its use). The warnings also included several accounts of various magic users that attempted the spell only to meet their immediate deaths.

Appendix IV

Glossary

A'ltal Bilv'at – a power of unknown origin or use, mentioned by Ahjiamed in 54,000 BC.

Alva'ci – A species of alien lifeform. Origin unknown. The term is also used to identify the singular creature that arrived on planet Earth in 54,000 BC (The Alva'ci).

Amulet, The – A transformation of the shard that enhances its power through a more perfect shape.

Ane'illuminus – One of the non-elemental powers. This power deals with the Mind/Thought. The wielder of this power can utilize the dreamscape and has precognitive dreams.

Seven Spells, The – One of the non-elemental powers. The wielder of this power can cast an assortment of spells. See Appendix I for a list of the spells and their uses.

Shard, The – A piece of orange rock from the cave in Yosemite that Hayden is stabbed with. The shard of rock becomes embedded in Hayden's side.

About the Author

Tony Contratto writes books, this much we know. In his free time, he is also a small business owner and nonprofit director. Tony's philosophy is that the most gripping and immersive fantasy tales happen in our imagination. In the spirit of that ideology, Tony spent several years formulating the story of his first novel within his head, before ever putting the proverbial pen to paper. Originally from Southern California, Tony now resides in Lake Havasu City, Arizona. Visit Tony at his website and follow him on social media at contrattos.net

Coming Soon

During a much-needed break from his continuous preparations, Abby and Dan helped Hayden brainstorm ideas to break through the plateau that was now plaguing his efforts. After a few hours of drinks at Eduardo Quesada's, the three friends had come up with and shot down dozens of ideas. Abby nonchalantly rolled an idea off her tongue that she was half sure would be just another proposal to add to the existential waste basket already full of them. Hayden paused and thought in silence for a few moments to ponder Abby's latest suggestion, stopping mid-sip of his beer before asking her to repeat herself and elaborate.

Join Hayden, Abby, and Dan as the *Agents of Fate Series*
continues with the second installment:

The Princess of Time

"...and the light shall mingle with the darkness, and together
they shall shine with a brilliance both dazzling and fearsome."

Sign up for the Agents of Fate email newsletter
and receive a FREE exclusive copy of
AOF: The Distant Shadow
at
agentsoffate.com
or
hensleydevere.com